PRAISE FOR TODD STRASSER

If I Grow Up

"Tight plotting and a crisp style will satisfy readers looking for nonstop action and plenty of urban drama."—*School Library Journal*

"Tough, authentic. . . . Strasser loads the book with startling true statistics, and the final pages are both hopeful and heartbreaking."
—*Booklist*

"Strasser deftly describes the desperation of inner-city life. . . . [His] writing puts the reader in the midst of the projects and offers totally real characters. . . . [R]iveting."—*VOYA*

Boot Camp

"The real-world issues will hit a nerve."—*Booklist*

"Teens . . . will be riveted by Garrett's appalling experiences and by his suspenseful escape. . . . A real eye-opener."—*KLIATT*

Can't Get There from Here

"Strasser's vibrant prose plunges readers into Maybe's hard life. . . . A very welcome addition to the slice-of-life genre in YA literature that may help to change some real lives."—*Kirkus Reviews*

"A story about people that we pretend don't exist. Strasser makes us l̶ _____

"Vivid, distres̶ _____ _ws_

★ "Both haunting and narrowing, the book deserves a wide readership, discussion, and debate."—*Booklist*, starred review

TODD STRASSER

SIMON & SCHUSTER BFYR

New York London Toronto Sydney New Delhi

SIMON & SCHUSTER BFYR

An imprint of Simon & Schuster Children's Publishing Division
1230 Avenue of the Americas, New York, New York 10020

This book is a work of fiction. Any references to historical events, real people, or real locales are used fictitiously. Other names, characters, places, and incidents are products of the author's imagination, and any resemblance to actual events or locales or persons, living or dead, is entirely coincidental.

SIMON & SCHUSTER BFYR is a trademark of Simon & Schuster, Inc.

For information about special discounts for bulk purchases, please contact Simon & Schuster Special Sales at 1-866-506-1949 or business@simonandschuster.com.

The Simon & Schuster Speakers Bureau can bring authors to your live event. For more information or to book an event, contact the Simon & Schuster Speakers Bureau at 1-866-248-3049 or visit our website at www.simonspeakers.com.

Also available in a SIMON & SCHUSTER BFYR hardcover edition

Book design by Lucy Ruth Cummins
The text for this book is set in Bembo.
Manufactured in the United States of America
First SIMON & SCHUSTER BFYR paperback edition February 2013
10 9 8 7 6 5 4 3 2 1
The Library of Congress has cataloged the hardcover edition as follows:
Strasser, Todd.
Famous / Todd Strasser.—1st ed.
p. cm.
Summary: Sixteen-year-old Jamie Gordon had a taste of praise and recognition at age fourteen when her unflattering photograph of an actress was published, but as she pursues her dream of being a celebrity photographer, she becomes immersed in the dark side of fame.
ISBN 978-1-4169-7511-3 (hc)
 [1. Fame—Fiction. 2. Actors and actresses—Fiction. 3. Paparazzi—Fiction. 4. Stalking—Fiction. 5. Hollywood (Los Angeles, Calif.)—Fiction.] I. Title.
PZ7.S899Fam 2011
[Fic]—dc22
2009048163
ISBN 978-1-4424-5418-7 (pbk)
ISBN 978-1-4424-1727-4 (eBook)

To Meg and Steven

Acknowledgments
My thanks to Jake Halpern for laying
some of the groundwork.

FAMOUS

EVERYBODY'S A DREAMER AND
EVERYBODY'S A STAR.

—"Celluloid Heroes" by the Kinks

01002 8.8 ISO AUTO

WHAT DO YOU IMAGINE WHEN YOU THINK ABOUT BEING FAMOUS?
Your photo on *omg!* and *TMZ?* Or on the cover of
People? That long white limousine gliding to a stop before
a crowd of adoring fans? The blinding caress of flashing
cameras? The eager outstretched hands offering photos
and scraps of paper for your autograph? Do you imagine
strolling up the red carpet? The doors that open only
for you? The embrace of the world? The admiration and
envy . . . everyone craving and wanting you?

The you, you, you of it all?

But you know, don't you, that what you imagine is an
illusion? Just a frail, fleeting flower offered up by a vast,

thorny jungle? Yes, you know about fame because you've read the magazines and seen all those stars on TV and on the Web. But that's only the flower, only the part they want you to see. It's not the reality. There's so much they don't let you see. The needle-sharp thorns. The climbing, choking vines. The hungry, sucking roots.

Or maybe you're one of those people who doesn't really *want* to know. You prefer the fantasy. Just the flower, please. Fame as you imagine it. The mansions, private yachts and jets, all those adoring fans, all that attention. All that you, you, you. Because you really don't care about the reality. It's not your problem because they're them and you're you. And even though the magazines say *They're Just Like Us!* they're not really. They're prettier, smarter, richer, and, to be brutally honest, just better.

Oops! I said it, didn't I? That they're better than you. And better than me.

Sucks, doesn't it? That deep down you believe they must be better, different, special. They *have* to be better.

Because they're famous.

And you're not.

But maybe that's not the whole truth either.

Maybe the truth is, they're no better than you or me or anyone else.

Then why do we think they are?

Perhaps because we want to. We *need* to.

Suppose I told you that I was once famous. People on the street recognized me. They asked for my autograph and wanted me to pose for photos with them.

Suppose I told you that there were stories about me in magazines and newspapers, and interviews on TV. On *network* TV, not that cheesy joke that passes for your local news and weather channel.

Suppose I told you that for a brief period of time photographers and videographers followed me everywhere, taking my picture and filming me, posting the shots and footage on the celebrity gossip sites and publishing the photos in the tabloids.

Cool, huh? Being famous like that. All that attention. All those people knowing who I was. All that me, me, me.

Can you imagine?

Only, whatever you imagine is so not the way it really is.

Suppose I told you that I hung out with one of the most famous stars in all of Hollywood? A name known by everyone who hasn't spent the past twenty years in some cave in Siberia. I stayed at her mansion, and we shopped and partied together. We hung around her pool and gossiped about hair and clothes and guys. We went to the homes of other huge stars and to the after-hours clubs only the superfamous can get into.

Suppose I told you that I knew her secrets.

Suppose I told you that she knew mine.

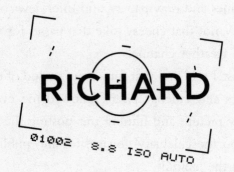

RICHARD

01002 8.8 ISO AUTO

Dear Willow,
   You still have not answered any
of my letters maybe it is hard for
someone as famous as you to find
the time to read letters. Maybe
Doris reads my letters and does not
tell you about them. But there is
a reason why I think you should
answer this letter it is because you
saw me today outside Sheen. I was
the one on the sidewalk with the

Angels baseball cap. You smiled at me remember it was when all those idiots were taking your picture and asking for your autograph. I was the one who did not ask you for nothing. I just waved and said, Have a nice day. That was when you smiled at me. I know you have to remember me.

I have been writing letters to you because I know you have felt my love and concern for you is why you smiled at me. You could feel our connection. We connect in a way that no one else understands I know that you have to let them take your picture and sign autographs because it is your job. But I know that what you really want is for someone to take care of you and protect you from all those people who want to hurt you.

It makes me angry the way they dont protect you better you have to be more careful that big bald head guy with the diamond in his ear is useless. Dont you know that when you are in a crowd like that he cant protect you? Anyone could step right past him and shove a knife in your heart if you had me beside you I would make sure that never happens. I promise I would always be there whenever people looked at pictures of you in magazines and on TV I would be there so they would know you were protected.

You should be more careful and stop taking these risks if something happened to you I dont know what I would do. All those people who want your picture and autograph just want things from you. They take and take and this hurts you I know I dont want nothing. I am the only one who wants to protect you.

I am sure you will write back to me when you get this letter because you smiled at me today. You felt our connection. I am so happy that you finally know who I am it is the first step to the day we are together forever and then you will be safe.

Love Forever

Richard

I OPEN MY EYES.

I am lying on a bare mattress in a bedroom I've never seen before. The mattress has that slightly chemical smell of newness. I am still wearing the jeans and spaghetti-strap top from the party last night. Sunlight floods through the uncovered window. Squinting, I sense from the angle of the California sun that it is early afternoon.

I am sixteen years old, a high school sophomore, on a week-long photo assignment 2,779 miles from home. Is it strange that someone can be a professional photographer at sixteen? I don't know why it should be. My agent says I've got a natural eye, a gift. I've even been called a prodigy. Does it feel odd to wake up in the middle of the afternoon in a strange bedroom? A room where the only piece of furniture is this bare mattress. No curtains, no chairs, no dresser. Did someone start to decorate it and then forget?

Or just get bored?

It doesn't matter. I've been in LA for seven days, living in a world where the things that usually matter don't seem to matter at all. Time, age, money, parents, school—none of those things means anything here. Is that really the way things are in LA?

No, not really.

It's just the way they are when you're staying at Willow Twine's Hollywood mansion.

IT STARTED WITH A CAMERA AND A COFFEE SHOP.

No, that's not right. Any shrink will tell you it started way before that. Like, when my brother Alex developed muscular dystrophy around the age of three, and five years later when my parents got divorced, and all that deep, twisted psychological gobbledygook.

But that camera, a black Nikon P90 with a 24x zoom lens, a fourteenth-birthday present from my father, was the charm that changed everything. It was the bridge I crossed from being a typical, everyday eighth grader to someone completely different.

An atypical eighth grader. A slightly almost-famous

eighth grader. Not that it was my plan. It just happened.

The day was gray, wet, and chilly. The outdoor light muted, shadowless, robbing my shots of contrast. The coffee shop was called Cafazine, and it provided two of life's great pleasures—coffee and gossip. Inside, the warm air was pungent with the scent of espressos, lattes, and cappuccinos. The gossip came in the form of magazines, tabloid newspapers, and wall-mounted HD screens tuned 24/7 to the celebrity channels. As I stood in line, my gaze drifted over to the shelves and racks filled with dog-eared glossies and wrinkled tabloids. All the covers featured variations on the same story:

ODD COUPLE! WILL BAD BOY REX
KILL WILLOW'S GOOD GIRL CAREER?
WHAT CAN WILLOW TWINE BE THINKING?
STUDIO EXECS WORRIED ABOUT REX'S BAD INFLUENCE!

As the entire world now knew, the adorable teen singing and acting sensation Willow Twine had recently fallen in with the heavily tattooed rock-'n-roll rogue Rex Dobro. The magazine covers showed the couple nestling on a blanket at the beach and loaded with shopping bags on Rodeo Drive. The gossip shows and websites led with a new angle on the love affair each evening, and even the late-night television hosts were making wisecracks.

After a quick scan of the headlines, I turned my attention to a tall woman in front of me holding the hand of a small, towheaded boy. She was wearing a long gray raincoat, wide-brimmed hat, and sunglasses, and recognition struck like a bolt from above—it was Tatiana Frazee, the supermodel! I'd seen enough pictures of her in magazines and on TV to know. Besides, why would anyone *not* famous wear a hat and big sunglasses inside on a cloudy day?

The boy was additional evidence. He was Conner Frazee, Tatiana's son with the fashion photographer Clayton Rodbart. Conner was tugging at his mother's gloved hand and pointing at a large blond brownie with chocolate chips inside the glass counter.

"I want that, Mommy!" he whined.

"Not before dinner," Tatiana answered firmly with a Germanic accent—yet another piece of evidence that supported my hunch.

"But I want it!" Conner persisted.

Other people on line glanced at the elegant woman, but they merely appeared annoyed by the boy's whining.

"I said no," Tatiana repeated.

"Yes!" The boy pulled at the gloved hand again.

"No," Tatiana replied icily through her teeth. Her dark glasses turned in my direction, and I quickly looked away. The code of behavior for a hip New York City prep school student required pretending that seeing someone famous was no big deal, especially when some of my friends and classmates had pretty famous parents of their own.

Still, having recognized Tatiana in Cafazine, it was impossible not to feel just a little bit awed. I reached into the pocket of my hoodie and fingered my new Nikon.

By now Tatiana and Conner had reached the counter.

"What would you like, ma'am?" the young man by the cash register asked. As the supermodel turned away from her son to answer, Conner suddenly yanked her hand as hard as he could.

Tatiana Frazee lost her balance and toppled forward, banging her perfect chin on a display of CDs, sending them crashing.

To this day I don't know what compelled me to yank the camera from my pocket and slide the shutter into quick-shot mode just in time to catch Tatiana, her sunglasses askew on her face, as she wheeled around and slapped Conner on the cheek.

The next shots caught Tatiana glaring at me with a mixture of horror and fury. An instant later she scooped Conner up under her arm and charged out of the shop.

A photo agent friend of my dad's sold the shots to a tabloid and to a website that specialized in celebrities' most embarrassing moments. A few weeks later I received a check for what seemed like a fortune to a fourteen-year-old.

Just for taking some pictures.

THE APARTMENT ON FIFTH AVENUE WILL FEEL COLD AND LIFELESS.

The oil paintings hang in perfect alignment, the silk pillows placed with exactness on the couches, each window shade drawn to precisely the same height. You will sit on the couch, your hands compressed between your knees, feeling nervous and uncomfortable. In the middle of what often seems like the noisiest city in the world, this vast apartment will feel deathly still.

A door will open, and Avy's mother will come through it carrying a white cardboard FedEx box. She will move stiffly in her tastefully plain black dress and single string of pearls, her face pale with just a trace of makeup, her neat dark hair falling to her shoulders. She will look nothing like the glamorous corporate lawyer you've met in the past.

Mrs. Tennent will sit down on the couch kitty-corner to you, her knees pressed together demurely, the box resting on her lap, her eyes red-rimmed and downcast. She will attempt a weak smile, but it is merely a ghost of one, like something left over from a former life.

You will both look at the box—open at one end—on her lap, and then your eyes will meet.

"You'll be careful with this?" she will ask.

"I promise," you'll reply.

"You were his closest friend."

At the funeral, Mrs. Tennent told you about the package that had arrived from California. Knowing how close he and you were, she had offered to let you borrow it for a while.

Now she will look down at the box in her lap. "It's all we have from this past year."

"I won't keep it too long."

Avy's mother will breathe in deeply and exhale regret like someone who has fought long and hard before deciding to surrender and let go. She will hold the box out to you, and you will take it.

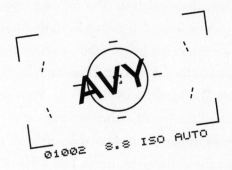

BET YOU NEVER SAW THE **ENTOURAGE** EPISODE where Johnny Drama decides he needs calf implants, but believe me, it's a classic. And so completely true! You're not going to get an underwear ad or beach scene if your legs are twigs. This is my third trip to Dr. Varga's clinic in Tijuana. He did my nose, my chin, and the liposuction. I totally trust him, and he charges about a third of what it would cost in LA.

But this is my last visit. Jamie's right. I've gotten into a messed-up scene out here in La-La Land. As soon as I get my new calves, I'm going home to New York to get cleaned up and healthy. Maybe start with some commercial work and then gradually get back into acting. After all, that's where I got my start, right? And I could've made it, too, if it hadn't been for my whacked-out, uptight parents.

And then, the next time I come out here I'll do it right. I won't be some kid with a head shot and a couple of cereal ads under his belt. I'll be an accomplished stage actor, fresh from a hit run on Broadway, or Shakespeare in the Park, or some edgy HBO or Showtime series. Next time it'll be because they're begging me to come. The heads of movie companies will send private jets. I'll be met on the runway by limos half a block long and whisked off to the hottest restaurants for meetings with top producers and directors.

That's how it's gonna be next time—the whole world will know it.

TEXT TO NASIM

01002 8.8 ISO AUTO

N,
Dad's driving me 2 JFK 2 catch the am flt 2 LA.
I'm so SRY re: last night. UR right. Maybe we do
focus 2 much on me and not enough on U. But I
hope U can understand that I was . . . I AM . . .
crazy/nervous/stressed re: going by myself on
this huge assignment. I promise 2 focus more
on U when I get back. UR the best BOYF anyone
ever had. I just feel like this is my big chance &
I'm TTLY scared I'll blow it. U can understand,
can't U? UR probably still asleep. By the time
U read this I'll be in the air. Hit me back, OK? I
really need 2 hear from U. XOXOXO Jamie

JAMIE

01002   8.8 ISO AUTO

THE GURGLE OF THE POOL FILTER AND A CHUCKLING LAUGH

float in through the open window above the mattress where I lie. My assignment, *A Week in the Life of Willow Twine*, is almost over. Or is this only the beginning? Should I even bother going back to New York? The young actors and actresses I photograph are out here doing TV and movies. New York is for older, more established stars—those who have time to do theater and don't have to be available to rush to a casting call. New York is my home, but it feels like the past. LA looks more and more like my future. And now that I've become friends with Willow and have met all these other stars through her, it would be an easy transition, except for

1. Losing Nasim, which will break my heart.
2. My mother, who predicted I'd want to stay out here and will throw an "I told you so" fit the size of Mount Olympus. Dad will be cool with it. He understands. You do what you have to do for your career. If you don't, someone else will and you'll miss your opportunity.

I sit up. Is it my imagination, or is the light from outside brighter than on past days? Maybe my eyes are overly sensitive because I'm semiseriously sleep deprived? Whatever the reason, I turn away from the window and look at the bare off-white bedroom walls. I am in the back of Willow's pink twenty-three-room Mediterranean-style palazzo, which once belonged to Madonna. And, before that, to Barbra Streisand. I wonder how many of my classmates know who Barbra Streisand is. Or the owner before her, Lana Turner. Who? Only the biggest movie starlet of the 1950s.

Funny how this mansion has been owned by a series of super famous (in their time) Hollywood starlets, all of whom had major difficulty with relationships.

I tug my fingers through the rat's nest that is my hair and get caught on a knot. Lying on the floor are my new Manolos, red alligator pumps that cost more than most cameras and are without question the most beautiful shoes ever to embrace my ugly feet. How could I refuse when Willow insisted on buying them for me?

Wait a minute. . . . Speaking of cameras, where's my Nikon? Oh my god! Where's my camera?

New York Weekly

THE YOUNGEST PAPARAZZO

The last bell rings, and the academic day at the exclusive downtown Herrin School is officially over. Jamie Gordon's friends leave for their after-school activities—music, dance, gymnastics, chess. Jamie, fifteen, a ninth-grader, heads for a different sort of after-school activity—one that involves hanging around outside a restaurant on Seventeenth Street in Chelsea, waiting with a dozen other paparazzi to see if Gabrielle Bloom, the star of the HBO series *Tugboat Annie*, will emerge with her new boyfriend, investment banker David Balkan.

If they do, Jamie will do her best to get the money shot.

Other parents have to pay for their children's after-school activities, but so far this year, Jamie has grossed close to $3,000. Her celebrity photos have appeared in half a dozen magazines as well as on numerous websites. She is universally regarded as the youngest paparazzo New York has ever seen.

"I really don't like being called a paparazzo," Jamie said on a recent afternoon while she waited with her fellow photographers on the sidewalk outside Chez Toi, where a tipster had said Bloom and Balkan were dining. "I consider myself a celebrity photographer."

While some might argue that she's splitting hairs, most of the photographers who work alongside Jamie say that she displays uncommon poise and professionalism for someone so young.

"Honestly, I'm amazed by the quality of her work," said photo agent Carla Harris, who reps Jamie's photos to the media. "A lot of people assumed that those shots of Tatiana Frazee were just luck. But the work Jamie's done since then has convinced me that she's both committed to this business and has the talent to succeed in it."

While none of Jamie's recent shots have equaled the now infamous photos of the supermodel Frazee losing her composure in a Soho coffee shop, Harris says that Jamie has been tenacious and consistent in her production of celebrity pictures.

"No one hits a home run every time," said Harris. "Jamie's okay with hitting singles and doubles. And that means that sooner or later she'll probably hit another home run."

Some of Jamie's fellow photogs are less charitable. "She's just a kid who lives at home. Every time she sells a picture, she's taking bread out of the mouths of guys like me who are trying to make a living," said one paparazzo who asked not to be identified.

"Face it," said another. "There's nothing really exceptional about her photos. If she were twenty-four instead of fifteen this would be a total nonstory."

But others offer grudging praise. "Jamie definitely has a knack for knowing where to set up and when to click the shutter," says videographer David Axelrod. "In this business, what counts is being able to anticipate a star's next move. I don't know how she figured it out so fast. Guess she's a quick study."

Jamie may be a quick study with a camera, but her mother, Dr. Carol Gordon, would prefer it if she were studying something else. "What she's doing is unusual and exciting, but it can't replace an education," said Dr. Gordon, who is a dentist. She and Jamie's father, Seth Gordon, a creative director at Shandler Advertising, divorced about five years ago.

"Jamie's curfew is eight o'clock on weekdays and eleven on weekends," said Dr. Gordon. "If her GPA falls below A-minus, that could easily change."

Jamie's father, Seth, takes a somewhat more laissez-faire attitude toward his daughter. "Obviously I'm biased, but I think Jamie's very mature for her age," said Mr. Gordon. "I trust her judgment. I was blown away when they wanted to send her out to Utah to cover the Sundance Film Festival. If it were up to me, I would have let her go."

But Jamie's mother put her foot down. "I didn't want her to miss school," said Dr. Gordon.

Speaking of which, what do the folks at Herrin think of Jamie's after-school career?

"We have many talented young people here," said headmistress Pamela Wickersham. "To be honest, I wasn't aware that Jamie was selling photographs to the media, but I'm not surprised. Herrin students are encouraged to pursue a wide range of extracurricular activities. Our job is to encourage and foster the pursuit of excellence in whatever fields interest our students."

When asked why she spends her afternoons and weekends hanging around restaurants and clubs waiting to photograph celebrities, Jamie said, "This may sound strange, but it's actually fun and exciting. It's cool if I make some money, but that's not really why I do it. There's something rewarding about getting a good shot. It's kind of like fishing. You go to a spot and wait and wait. Sometimes nothing bites. But once in a while you catch a fish."

And perhaps that's the answer. If Jamie Gordon lived near a lake, she might spend her time waiting for a trout to bite. But living in New York, she has no choice but to troll for a different sort of game.

"YOU'RE FAMOUS." THE SPEAKER OF THOSE WORDS WAS MY boyfriend, Nasim. It was the first time anyone ever said that to me, and I had to admit that it felt good. Right up there with "You're pretty" or "You're smart." No, even *better* than "You're smart."

"Thank you," I replied.

"You're welcome." Nasim was Persian and a sophomore at Herrin. He was tall and thin, yet broad shouldered, with long, straight black hair, olive skin, and the darkest almond-shaped eyes I've ever seen. Personally, I thought he was the best-looking boy at Herrin.

At the moment of Nasim's proclamation about my

fame, we were hurrying along the sidewalk toward school, clutching paper cups of cappuccinos, and dodging the briefcase crowd trudging toward the subway to work. Nasim reached into his backpack and pulled out a copy of *New York Weekly*. "How many people do we know who have been profiled in a major magazine? New York City's youngest paparazzo ever? I believe the correct answer would be one."

I grabbed his arm to stop him and we kissed in the middle of the crowded sidewalk, our lips pressed warmly as other bodies brushed past. "Thank you," I said, our faces close. "Only, for the six hundred and seventy-fifth time, I am not a paparazzo. I am a celebrity photographer."

Nasim rolled his gorgeous almond eyes, and we started to hurry again, our shoulders now and then bumping. "There is no difference."

"There's a *big* difference," I insisted. "I may take pictures of celebrities, but I don't stalk or harass them or try to get them to punch me so that I can sue them for assault."

Nasim changed the subject. "You never told me they wanted to send you to the Sundance Film Festival."

"I don't know why my father had to bring that up," I said, although the truth was, I knew *exactly* why he'd done it: to bask, as they say, in the reflected glory of his daughter's accomplishments. "I'm not exactly proud that my mother wouldn't let me go. I mean, do you think that in the entire history of independent film festivals, there's ever been anyone else who had to say no because her mother didn't want her to miss school?"

By now we were nearing the "hip, downtown," but still academically excellent Herrin School, which our parents paid a fortune to so that we could get in to the best colleges and someday become rich and important and genetically prodigious. As we joined the ranks of our fellow movers and shakers to be, Nasim leaned close and whispered in my ear. "Don't look now, but at least one hundred people are staring at you."

I would be lying if I didn't admit the thrill that ran through me.

We pushed through the wooden front doors into the warm, perfume-scented, emotionally charged world of Children of Privilege Trying Not to Appear Too Chic and headed for our lockers. Uncertain how to deal with the attention, I felt my face flush in response to the glances and whispers.

"And what must be most exciting of all for you?" Nasim said. "That you are in the same magazine as your favorite couple, Willow Twine and Rex Dobro."

He was right. If there is such a thing as Fame by Proximity, then I was doubly blessed and privately delighted to be in the same issue that carried an article about the break-ups, the make-ups, and the shake-ups of Rexlow, Hollywood's hottest couple. Recently, hardly a week had gone by without some report of a spat or fight, tearful reconciliation followed by an expensive truce offering. Rex gave Willow diamond rings, bracelets, and necklaces. She gave him fast cars, motorcycles, and a Jet Ski. One thing no one doubted was, they were crazy in love with each other.

With the emphasis on "crazy."

"Oh my god! Kickin' story, Wonder Girl!" Coming toward us was Avril Tennent, the nicest, sweetest, cutest chubby-guy-with-curly-brown-hair-who-was-convinced-he-was-going-to-be-famous someday that you'd ever want to meet.

Postgush, Avy turned to Nasim and bumped knuckles. "Yo, dawg."

"S'up, pup?" replied Nasim. It was some sort of semi-private inside joke they shared, a running satire on the macho school jocks who always greeted one another in a similar fashion.

Avy turned back to me. "Do you know what this means? You, Jamie Gordon, are, at this moment, the most famous high school student in all of New York! So now we can be famous together! You and me! I mean, you're in this week's *New York Weekly*! This is amazing. Mind-boggling! How does it feel?"

"Pretty cool," I said, as his words floated though my thoughts. *You, Jamie Gordon, are, at this moment, the most famous high school student in all of New York!*

I liked the sound of it. What's the point of pretending? To be honest, it felt fabulous. Can you imagine? People all over the city. Thousands. Maybe even millions. People I didn't even know. All of them knew who I was.

We talked a little more and then at the next corner, Avy headed in a different direction saying he'd catch us later. Nasim and I continued down the hall. If the hallway that morning had been something of an obstacle course, I wondered if it was about to become a minefield. Planted in the middle of the corridor directly in front of us, chatting amicably and pretending to be totally unaware that they were forcing everyone to go around them, was Shelby "The Lioness" Winston and her pride.

We've all seen enough teen movies and *Gossip Girl* to be familiar with Shelby. I suppose what truly puzzled me was how someone like her could go through life without realizing that she was the stereotypical rich, snotty, popular girl. So either she didn't see it in herself, or she saw it and had made a conscious decision that she'd rather be rich, snotty, and popular than rich, snotty, and unpopular.

On the other hand, I have a feeling Shelby would be the first to point out that I also fit a familiar stereotype— the sort-of maybe sometimes semipopular, sort-of artsy, sort-of pretty, sort-of-just slightly pudgy, sort-of-always questioning, sort-of-uncertain-about-a-lot-of-things type who probably grows up to write the very books and movies about girls like Shelby that I just referred to.

But here's the truth. And I know some people will despise me for this, but I'm just being as honest as I can possibly be. From the very instant that I learned *New York Weekly* was going to do a piece on me, I couldn't help wondering how one person in particular would react. I mean, here I was, living in one of the great power, money, and media capitals of the world. By now the story in *New York Weekly* had probably been read, and my picture seen, by millions of people, some of them incredibly important—movie stars who made their homes in New York, the mayor, probably someone on the New York Yankees, perhaps a senator or two, surely the odd Rockefeller and Clinton. *I knew* this kind of publicity is way bigger than high school. *I knew* that someday I'd look back at Herrin and wonder how I could have possibly cared what anyone there thought. And yet, no matter how hard I tried, there was one person besides Nasim and Avy whose opinion was going to count. And that person was . . . Shelby Winston.

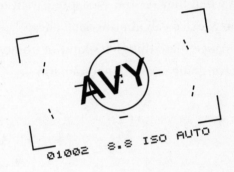

CAN'T SAY I'M THRILLED ABOUT GOING BACK EAST AFTER I HAVE my calves done. Out here it's so different. Everybody has cosmetic work. Everybody! It's like orthodontia. Had liposuction? Got a new nose? Chin? Some Botox? No one even blinks. Back in New York everyone has surgery too, but it's all hush-hush. No one wants anyone to know. People disappear for a month and then reappear with a new nose and think no one will figure it out? Give me a break.

Some of the kids from Herrin probably won't even recognize me, but some will, and people are bound to make comments, right? So who cares? Love me, love my new look, okay? Besides, I am so past that high school scene. Those kids who still live with their parents, what do they know? They're just tots.

But then there are my parents. Can't imagine what they'll do when they see me. Not sure I want to imagine.

Even in Mexico calf implants ain't cheap. But there are ways to finance these things. It's kind of ironic, but those ways involve going across the border, too.

N,
1st time in 1st class! The steward gave me Coke in a REAL glass *before* we even backed from the gate!

First it was me and Actor Man wearing a silver gray suit. I'm sure I've seen him on TV. Next on was a woman in red high heels with Louis Vuitton beauty case. Then came woman #2 in black pants suit and stylish glasses, talking on a BlackBerry. Then 2 scruffy guys/jeans and sneakers. Carrying leather satchels stuffed with papers. SCREENWRITERS?

The last to arrive was RACHEL MCEWEN! That's right, the STAR!!!! N, UVE seen her! She's got at least 1 Oscar and nominated a bunch of other times. She sat with personal assistant—chubby woman lugging 2 carry-on bags. Everyone in 1st class tried not 2 stare.

During the flight the other passengers paid homage to Rachel. If they'd met her before (Actor Man and black pants suit lady), they reminded her of when and where. If they didn't know her, they introduced themselves and expressed admiration for her work. It was like Queen Rachel giving audience to her subjects!

WELCOME TO HOLLYWOOD!

At LAX 2 men in dark suits and sunglasses were waiting for Rachel at the gate. (How did they get through security?) They escorted her and her assistant through the terminal.

Dozens of heads turned. People asked for autographs. The dark suits stayed close. I think Rachel enjoyed the attention. Outside the terminal a long white limousine waited. The driver held the door. Just before Rachel got in, she looked around. . . . Hoping someone would ask for just 1 more autograph?

She left, and Zach picked me up in a Honda (Where's MY limo? ;-). He works for Willow. Hello LA—sun, palm trees! Smoggy air that makes your eyes burn. I can't believe I'm here!

Movie billboards everywhere. Entire walls of buildings covered by enormous faces of stars. We drove up into the hills, past palms and lush green tropical growth, and stopped outside a tall iron gate. Beyond the gate and vast green lawn was a huge sunlit pink stucco mansion. Zach punched a code and we went through. A very large man with a very big frown was waiting in front of the mansion. I got out of the car, and he said, "ID please."

Luckily I had my Herrin ID. Then he pointed at my bag and said, "Any weapons or drugs?"

Can you believe it? That was my welcome to Willow's. More later. How did you spend first day of vacation? (See? I'm interested!) Miss you. Like, tons. Hit me back. xoxoxo

YOU WILL LOCK THE DOOR TO YOUR ROOM AND TURN ON SOME music. Something soft and emo. A single voice accompanied by a piano or guitar. You will sit on your bed, listening to the melancholy tune, and stare at the FedEx box for a long time. The room, lit only by the small lamp on your night table, will feel dim and shadowy like a burrow, a safe place to hide. And yet you will feel afraid. Afraid to look inside. Afraid to learn what it will tell you about the end of your friend's life. Afraid that somehow you were partly responsible.

And yet from the moment Mrs. Tennent told you about the box, you knew you had to see what it contained. As if it might possess the answers to all the questions you wished you could still ask Avy. So after a while, even though you're still not feeling ready, you will reach down, bend back a flap, and feel an instant of relief that the first thing you see is not a photograph of Avy near the end.

Instead you will find a memory stick attached to a green and yellow lanyard. Curious, you will plug it into your MacBook and discover that it holds only one file, a video. The thought of playing it will frighten you. Your fingers will tremble and your heart will thump against your sternum. What if this video is something you really don't want to see?

But you will play it. A picture will come on the screen—an unrecognizable blur. It's someone very close to the camera, moving, probably setting up the shot. As the person backs away, you will see that it's Avy in a room with an unmade bed and posters taped crookedly to the walls. He will sit in a chair, brush his dyed straightened black hair back with his fingertips, look at the camera, and ask, "What was the biggest surprise you faced after moving to LA from New York?"

You will watch as he settles back in the chair, gazes up at the ceiling as if pondering his own question, then looks back at the camera. "Probably discovering that there were already hundreds of guys just like me out here trying to get the same acting jobs I was auditioning for. I mean, I'm not stupid. I knew before I left New York that there'd be competition. But I never expected to be sent to an audition and find two dozen other slightly chubby guys with curly brown hair and freckles. It was like ever since Seth Rogen and Jonah Hill, every chubby curly-haired guy in the world thought he could be a star."

Avy will nod and smile, obviously pleased with his answer. You will imagine that he must have been practicing for an interview he was going to give. Now he leans forward and asks, "Did you always know you wanted to become an actor?"

He will cross ankle over knee and answer. "Not really. It wasn't like I was born totally focused on acting. When I was younger I was into sports and music and video games like every other kid. But going to private school in New York City makes it hard to excel in sports. You don't get the playing time or access to fields. I remember in summer camp they said I had a good arm, but the rest of the year I hardly even saw a baseball diamond, unless we went to a Yankees game. Who knows? Maybe if I'd gone to one of the suburban schools I'd be throwing for the Yankees today."

The fog of sadness will thicken around you. No hint of irony accompanies your friend's assertion that he could have been good enough to play for the greatest professional baseball team ever. This was Avy, who stood barely five feet nine inches tall and, as far as you knew, never displayed an ounce of athletic talent. Yes, you'd always known that the chances of him actually becoming a big star were slim. But doesn't everyone who wants to be famous have to be slightly unrealistic? When did Avy's dreams become delusions of grandeur?

RICHARD

01002 8.8 ISO AUTO

Dear Willow,

I dont understand why you have
not written back to me. I know you
know who I am because you smiled
at me that day outside Sheen I
was the only one wearing an Angels
baseball cap. Do you know why I
wear it? It is not because I am a
baseball fan it is because I am your
guardian angel.

I dont understand why you are
not more careful. In the magazines

and on the computer I see photos of you shopping and coming out of restaurants. Dont you understand how easy it would be for someone to hurt you? Is it that you dont think anyone would want to hurt you? That is wrong! You dont know what kind of people there are in this world. They know that if they hurt you everyone will know who they are. He could become famous just for hurting you. There are people like that. You have to believe me because I know.

You should write back to me. You know who I am. You should be more careful. I could protect you. I would always be at your side and never let anything bad happen to you.

Your guardian angel

Richard

I KNOW IT'S LAME THAT I CARED ABOUT SHELBY WINSTON'S OPINION, but at least give me credit for being honest and keeping it in perspective. I mean, welcome to high school, right?

There in the Herrin hallway on that Monday morning after the *New York Weekly* article came out in the fall of my freshman year, Shelby Winston clamped her eyes on me. There was a time, back in sixth or seventh grade, when her gaze alone would have caused my pulse to race and my face to burn. But that was then. Now I managed a friendly smile. Shelby smiled back and said, "Can I have your autograph?"

I felt myself stiffen. Was she making fun of me, or was

this just a cute way of saying that maybe she *was* just an eensy weensy bit impressed? The only thing I knew for certain was that she didn't really want my autograph.

"Seriously," she said. "Congratulations." And the girls who'd collected around her like iron shavings clinging to a magnet all nodded in agreement. Shelby glanced at Nasim beside me and raised a curious eyebrow.

"This is Nasim Pahlavi," I said, and turned to him. "You know Shelby, don't you?"

"I've never actually had the pleasure." Nasim extended his hand. "Hello."

Shelby smiled and shook his hand. "The pleasure is mine."

Shelby's compliment may have been a highlight of what I've come to refer to as "my first minute of fame," but that didn't mean it was over. All day long kids, teachers, and administrators stopped to say that they were impressed, that they never knew.

And it didn't stop when the school day ended, either.

"What makes you think they'll let us in?" I asked Dad later that night. It was ten o'clock, and we were standing on line in the dark outside Club Gaia with Raigh, Dad's tall, blond squeeze du jour.

"You'll see," he replied. Ever since he divorced Mom he seemed happy living by himself while now and then dipping into an apparently bottomless well of stylish single career women in their early forties who wanted to get married and have children before the biological clock stopped ticking. They never stayed with Dad for long; as soon as they realized he had no interest in settling down, they were gone. I once asked him why he didn't find someone—and settle down. His answer: "What fun would *that* be?"

The line inched forward. It was a cool, breezy fall evening, and people wore light jackets and scarves. The entrance had no identifying marks—just a bare lightbulb over a plain green metal door. You'd never suspect there was a hot club there were it not for the enormous man with the twin earrings and sloping forehead guarding the door.

With only one couple ahead of us, I tugged Dad's sleeve and stood on my tiptoes so I could whisper in his ear without Raigh hearing. "Let's just go. There's no way they're going to let us in. This is going to be really embarrassing."

"I think we have a shot," he whispered back.

I knew what his plan was, and I knew it wouldn't work. Club Gaia was for the Famous. Not the "high school famous," not even the "child prodigy famous," but the Famous with a capital F as in movie and TV stars, best-selling authors, rock-'n-roll survivors from the sixties and seventies, and artists whose works hung in museums. If any mere mortals knew what the interior looked like, it was from photos that had appeared in *New York* magazine and *Vanity Fair.*

"It's fine if you want to humiliate yourself," I whispered. "But why bring me into it?"

"Just chill, honey." (I love my father, but I wish he wouldn't say that.)

After the couple ahead of us were rejected and had slunk away, we stepped forward into the glare of the lightbulb. Mr. Double Earrings pursed his lips and frowned the frown of nonrecognition. He was just beginning to shake his head when Dad pulled out a copy of *New York Weekly,* opened it to the story, then pointed from the magazine to me.

Not a word was spoken.

I groaned inwardly. *My own father was trying to use me as social currency, only he was about to find out that his money was no good here.*

The big man's eyes narrowed. He looked at the magazine, then at me. This was where the butterfly of fantasy went *splat* on the windshield of reality. Feeling the heat of humiliation begin to warm my face, I stared down at the sidewalk.

Dad's hand closed on my arm and gave it a little tug.

Next thing I knew, we were inside seated at a semicircular ottoman around a low table, with martinis for Dad and Raigh, a Diet Coke for me, and the scent of incense in the air. I was pretty sure the guy in the suit standing at the bar was one of the Marsalis brothers and that the blonde a few tables over once had a recurring role on *CSI*. Meanwhile, Dad was leaning toward the glamorous young couple to our right and showing them the *New York Weekly* article.

Was I being übersensitive, or was this totally bizarre?

"You're not going to the professional children's school," Mom said the next morning. The inspiration for this idea had come from Raigh the night before. A neighbor on her floor had a ballet dancer daughter who went to that school.

"Why not?" I asked with a yawn. "It would be perfect for me. And ninth grade's the perfect year to transfer."

"Herrin is perfect for you." Dressed in her work clothes, she was standing at the kitchen counter, waiting impatiently for her chai tea to steep. I was sitting at the kitchen table, head propped in my hands, watching a bowl of Cheerios go soggy.

"Herrin can't make the time accommodations I need for my career," I said.

The facial tic Mom sometimes got around her left eye fired involuntarily.

"Why do you hate it so much when I use that word?" I asked.

"I don't hate it."

"You soooo hate it. It's like in your opinion no one

who's fifteen can have a career. But there are Olympic skaters, gymnasts, tennis players, actors, and singers who do it all the time."

"That's different," she said.

"Oh, really?"

"Yes, really. Most of them are seizing a moment that may be the only opportunity they'll ever have. Young athletes have to take advantage of a youthful agility and flexibility they won't have when they're in their twenties. The actors and singers are capitalizing on being cute and adorable in a way that might very well change dramatically by the end of puberty."

"And you don't think I'm doing the same thing?" I asked.

Mom leveled her gaze at me. "I think you're talented and you've worked hard. I'm proud of you, Jamie, but honestly, just because you've sold some photographs and *New York Weekly* ran that story about you because you're so young does not mean this is a career. I'm not sure how you can call hanging around with a disreputable bunch of freelance photographers who make money by invading other people's privacy a career. No one ever mistook a paparazzo for an Olympic gymnast."

"They might if they saw some of the moves my 'disreputable' friends make to get a picture," I quipped with another yawn. "Why shouldn't car-dodging be an Olympic sport?"

I'd hoped Mom would smile, but she didn't. The skin

around her eyes wrinkled. "What time did you get home last night?"

"Don't change the subject," I said.

A healthy dose of motherly stink-eye followed as she fumed, "Today is a school day and you need to be awake. Your father is the most irresponsible excuse for an adult that ever—"

"We were celebrating."

The tooth puller looked blank. "Sorry?"

"The *New York Weekly* article? Hello? The one all about your daughter and the career she's not allowed to have?"

The kitchen door swung open, and Elena wheeled in Alex. My brother cannot speak or control his actions, and yet he is incredibly aware and astute. He took one look at my mother and me, and I could see in his eyes that he knew we'd been arguing.

He made a grunting sound and a jerky motion with his head. It was his way of saying, "What's going on?"

My mother and I locked eyes. "You'll have to forgive me if your *career* is not foremost on my mind," she said. "I have a few other things to attend to."

I KNOW IT SOUNDS LIKE A CLICHÉ, BUT I FEEL NAKED WITHOUT MY CAMERA. Or even worse than naked, since these days who cares if you're naked? The camera represents who I am. It's my identity. With it, I'm a sixteen-year-old celebrity photographer. (And maybe something of a celebrity myself?) Without it, who am I?

What am I?

The answers to these questions will have to wait. Right now I just need to find my Nikon. I try to remember last night. Not that it should be difficult; it's just that out here, day and night, and day after day, blend together into a sort of nonstop repetition of the same thing over and over again. Last night was a party. But even on nights when there's no "official" party there's a loose semiparty atmosphere. People come and go, appear and disappear—Willow's friends, gofers, security guard, personal assistant, therapist, masseur, agents, magazine photographer (me!), pool guy, gardeners, cook—in an unending looping parade.

As best as I can remember, I had my camera with me early this morning when I came upstairs to find a place to sleep. Before that I'd gone out to the guesthouse—where I'd been "assigned" when I first arrived earlier this week—but the door was locked, so I'd wandered back to the main house and found this room. Normally I would have put the camera on a night table or dresser, but since there is no furniture in the room, I left it on the floor beside the mattress, and close to the wall so I wouldn't accidentally step on it if I got up in the middle of the night, or day, or whatever.

So where is it? I check the bathroom. Not there either. I walk barefoot out into the hallway with the straps of the Manolos hooked through my fingers, then downstairs and out across the grassy lawn to the guesthouse (whoever locked me out last night has now left, leaving beer cans, cigarette butts, and an unmade bed) to put on a pair of sneakers. Leaving the guesthouse, I'm once again struck by the clarity of the air this morning. Perhaps I just didn't realize before how much the famous LA smog filtered and softened the light. But today every detail—every leaf, blade of grass, and ripple in the pool—feels extra crisp. If only I had my camera! I head toward the pool, where Zach, the house boy, and Daphne, the house techie, are straightening up from last night's frolic.

"Either of you see a camera?" I ask.

"Think I saw one on the kitchen counter," Zach says.

The kitchen counter? That's weird. I don't recall even being in the kitchen last night. I was mostly out around the pool.

Passing through the French doors, the aroma of fresh-brewed coffee is in the air, and there on the marble kitchen counter, where I swear I wouldn't—couldn't—have left it, is my Nikon.

"Buenos dìas, Miss Jamie. You like some breakfast?" Maria, the Mexican cook, hands me the mug of coffee she knows I crave. "Fresh fruit maybe? Eggs over easy?"

"Fresh fruit sounds great, thanks." I sit down at the counter and gaze out past the shimmering crystal blue pool to the unused tennis court, the perfect lawn, and the tall green hedge that hides the twelve-foot-high wall around the property.

Maria slides a bowl of fresh strawberries, pineapple, melon, and orange slices in front of me. I thank her and wonder if today will be any different from the previous days. To an easterner, the weather out here has an uncanny consistency, which only adds to the endless sameness.

The camera rests on the marble counter beside me while I sip my coffee. Now that it's back in my sight, my anxiety has evaporated. I didn't take many shots at the party last night. Willow asked me not to. Does that sound crazy? After all, I'm here on assignment, right? Document a week in Willow's life, they said.

But "they" are Willow's management, and "they" have made it clear that my assignment is to show the world the Willow Twine "they" want it to see—the sweet, girl-ish pop star (her true age, twenty-one, is a more closely guarded secret than the president's personal cell phone number) whose recent stint in rehab was due to an "accidental," "once in a lifetime" blunder, the "innocent mistake" of falling under the toxic spell of the rakishly handsome, extremely ne'er-do-well breaker of hearts, destroyer of hotel rooms, and wrecker of fast cars, Rex Dobro.

All I'd taken the previous night were a few innocent party shots—nothing that wouldn't fit comfortably on the *Christian Science Monitor's* website—and had intentionally not taken the shots that editors everywhere would have paid major league money for. As a result, this morning I'm in no rush to review what's in the camera's memory. I finish the fruit, take another long sip of coffee, and wonder if I can really make this idea of staying here in California work. It's not *that* crazy, is it? After all, Avy's done it. He's been out here for almost eight months trying to make it as an actor. (But where is he, anyway? I've been texting him all week and he hasn't answered.)

Most important, I've now got this huge opportunity. I've earned the trust of Willow Twine, one of the biggest stars in Hollywood. She's already introduced me to a bunch of her actor friends and has promised to hook me up with even more. If I stay, I have a chance to become the Annie Leibovitz of the LA young actor scene. I could grow with them. I could be their favorite go-to photographer for decades to come.

But what about Nasim? My insides clench and my heart corkscrews when I think of him and the fight we had before I left New York. I would so hate to lose him, but I know what my father would say: You're young, you can't let a guy influence the direction of your career. Back in New York, all I've got is this weird sort of slowly diminishing quasi-celebrity for being successful at such a young age. But in two or three years that won't matter anymore. By the time I'm eighteen I'll be just another shutterbug in a city teeming with them.

So, if I do decide to stay, that's got to be the argument I use—that my future is out here, where I have a real chance at having a lifelong career as a celebrity photographer. Like Avy, I can finish high school at the Los Angeles Professional Children's Academy and live in an apartment with a chaperone. It's all about who you know. And right now who I know is here in LA, not there in New York.

Bare feet pad along the floor behind me, and into the kitchen trudges Rex Dobro, the precise persona who, according to Willow's management, is seriously non grata in her life. The cause of her recent flirtation with ruin and rehab that nearly destroyed her career. And, as a result, he is the person whose reappearance in her life must be kept an absolute secret.

I can't help but feel shivers each time I see him. Rex is dangerously alluring, long and lanky, tattooed and pierced, dark stubble covering his chin, dark hair falling down his face, past his eyes, strands of beads and medallions hanging from his neck, leather and silver bracelets around his wrists. He enters the kitchen bare-chested, a pair of torn jeans hanging provocatively low on his skinny hips. Believe me, once you've met this man you won't blame Willow for her "innocent mistake." This is a guy whose animal magnetism is on par with the megagravity of a black hole.

Willow may be more famous, but Rex is way, way more thrilling.

"Hey," he mutters with a raffish smile as he slides onto the stool beside me, planting his elbows on the counter and running his fingers through his hair. Even though I myself have been featured in magazines and on TV, I cannot get used to the idea that I am sitting next to someone this famous, even if all he's really known for is drug abuse, on-stage brawls, hotel room destruction, and numerous arrests for assault, public lewdness, and disorderly conduct.

"Good morning, Mr. Rex," says Maria. "You like coffee?"

"Morning, Maria. Yeah, lots of it, strong and black." He turns to me. "How'd you sleep?"

Each time he levels his gaze at me I feel like I'm melting into a pool of jiggling goose flesh. "Okay, you?"

The smile increases, and he gets a dreamy look in his eyes. We both know where he spent last night (well, actually, this morning), and the look he gives me is just so sheepishly filled with wonder, delight, and happiness. Rex Dobro, animal magnetic love puppy.

If only the world knew. . . .

But the world must never know.

I like the contrast of what I'm seeing—the soft, relaxed happiness of Rex's face here in the kitchen set against the background of this morning's extra-bright light glinting off the surface of the pool.

"Hold that," I tell him, and reach for the camera. "Just one for my personal collection, okay? I swear no one will ever see it."

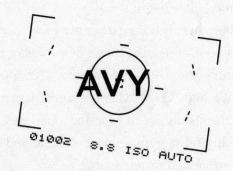

THEY CALL IT A TROLLEY, BUT IT'S REALLY A FIVE-CAR-LONG, modern electric street train. On board are maids, cooks, and gardeners headed home for family visits, tourists on day trips, amped college kids eager to sample the illicit pleasures on the other side of the border, and European adventurers lugging backpacks. The trolley also carries people like me, who would just as soon not say where we're going or why.

Tijuana only an hour's ride south from San Diego, and not the most comfortable when you've got thousands of dollars taped around your waist. And they always have the air-conditioning on way too high. We're only halfway there and already I'm shivering.

Good thing I only have to travel this way for the trip down. In a few weeks, when my new calves have healed, I'll catch a ride on a private yacht on its way back to America's Finest City from a fishing trip along the Baja. In the unlikely case that we get stopped by the Coast Guard or DEA, it'll look like I'm just some rich guy's kid. (Hey! Know what's funny? I actually *am* some rich guy's kid!) Anyway, I don't exactly fit the profile of a drug smuggler's mule. From San Diego I'll catch a bus to LA, deliver the goods to Bernie, and walk away with a new pair of calves all paid for. Not bad for less than three weeks' work.

And then I'll go back to New York, deal with my parents, and hang with Jamie.

E-MAIL TO
NASIM

01002   8.8 ISO AUTO

N,

Hi from La-La Land. No texts or e-mails from you :-(. Please write and don't be angry. Like you said last night, you can't expect me to know more about you if you don't tell me, right?

Anyway, I couldn't believe the man outside Willow's--his name is Sam--was serious. Weapons? Drugs? Sorry, just cameras.

The inside of Willow's mansion is all marble, glass, and dark wood. Lots of beautiful blue and yellow Spanish tile. I met Maria, the cook, and Daphne, who's in charge of everything technical, from the TVs and computers to Willow's BlackBerry. I'm staying in the guesthouse behind the mansion (there's also a pool house and a gardener's cottage--it's a HUGE property). I unpacked and took a walk around the pool, tennis court, and grounds. Then a large cream-colored Mercedes convertible pulled up in front, and Willow got out wearing a short white poofy dress with big bright flower patterns, cinched at the waist with a thick pink belt and a matching pink hair band. Zach grabbed red, blue, and yellow shopping bags out of the trunk. Willow blew kisses to two women in the car, then went inside, with Zach staggering behind with the shopping bags.

I went into the front room with Sam. Willow was going over her schedule for the rest of the day with Doris, her personal assistant, who looks like she's in her early thirties and is kind of dowdy. Willow shot me a high-voltage smile. "Jamie! I am so happy you're here."

Is it possible for human beings to

radiate? If so, Willow does it.

"I am dying to get in the pool," she said. "Let's go!"

Of course, what's the one thing I never thought of packing? A bathing suit. So Willow told Doris to call someone named Bobby at Le Tuc, then headed upstairs, saying she'd be back "in a flash."

After a while a green jaguar came up the driveway and a skinny guy wearing all black came in with a dozen swimsuits still on hangers. I picked the cheapest one-piece ($289!), plain black. When I tried to pay, the guy looked at me like he didn't know what money was.

I changed into the suit, and Willow <u>still</u> hadn't come downstairs. I guess here in La-La Land "a flash" is more like "the time it takes a glacier to travel across Greenland." Next a bright red Lexus convertible came up the driveway. The raven-haired driver got out. With a big frown Sam gestured at her shoulder bag, emptied its contents on the car's hood, and inspected them. The dark-haired woman had her hands on her hips, and even though she was wearing sunglasses, you could tell she was seriously PO'd.

Still waiting for an e-mail from you. Come on, N. You know how stressed I was last night. I said I'm sorry. xoxoxo

HERE'S ONE WAY TO TELL PRIVATE AND PUBLIC SCHOOLS APART.
At lunch in private school we sit in the dining room at
round tables covered with tablecloths.

I put my elbows on the table and yawned. "I wish they
served coffee."

"Where were you last night?" Avy asked as he spread 8
x 10 glossy color head shots out on the table before Nasim
and me. "I sent you about a thousand IMs and text messages."

"Club Gaia," I answered, and glanced at Nasim, who
was reading *The Brothers Karamazov* and didn't seem to
hear. Shouldn't it have been he who wanted to know
where I was last night and who sent a thousand IMs and

texts? Why hadn't I heard from him at all?

Avy jerked his head up and stared at me with wide-eyed astonishment. "No way!"

"Uh-huh. I would have hit you back, but my cell phone died."

The amazement in Avy's voice caught Nasim's attention. He looked up. "Sorry?"

"Dude, last night your girlfriend got in to the hottest club in all of New York, which basically means all of the East Coast, which basically means the hottest club between London and LA." Avy had a wonderful knack for exaggerating.

Nasim looked at me with a curiously raised eyebrow. A sign of mild jealousy, I hoped.

"I was with my dad and his last night's girlfriend," I explained.

"How did you get in?" Avy's expression went from astonishment to wonder.

"The *New York Weekly* article?" Nasim guessed. His astuteness could at times be otherworldly. Clearly he paid attention to a great deal more than one might have thought.

"Who did you see?" Avy asked eagerly.

I reeled off the names of the rich and famous who'd showed up after we arrived.

"Did anyone recognize you?" Nasim asked when I'd finished.

I shook my head.

"That's not fair." Avy came to my rescue. "She was totally out of context. If you'd put a camera around her neck and stuck her in the middle of a pack of paparazzi I bet ninety percent of the people at Gaia last night would have known who she was."

"Point well taken." Nasim nodded.

"I did get a couple of long, don't-I-know-you-from-somewhere looks," I said.

"Exactly. But enough about you." Avy swept his arm over the head shots he'd spread around the table: Avy in a dozen different poses, all looking back at us. A plethora of Avys. "Let's focus on me. You have to help me figure out which one to use."

"I like the one with you smiling," I said.

"I think you should use the serious one," said Nasim.

"We have to decide, guys," Avy said. "The American Movie and Television Academy convention is this weekend. I have to pick a shot and get a couple of hundred dupes for the agents, since my supergood friend Jamie won't use her connections to help me get one."

"That is so not true!" I gasped, feeling hurt. "I did too try to help you get an agent."

"Oh, right," Avy scoffed playfully. "Carla sent me to two talent scouts, and then she stopped answering my calls. Some people have to see twenty or thirty agents before they find one they connect with."

"Will there not be many aspiring actors just like you looking for agents at this convention?" Nasim asked.

"It's not about numbers," Avy said. "It's about desire. You've got to show them you want it. That you'll eat it, sleep it, *kill* for it. You know that Elijah Wood, Ashton Kutcher, and Constance Kelly were all discovered at the AMTA?"

From inside my bag came a vibrating buzz.

Avy checked his watch. "That would be Carla."

I held the cell phone under the table, where it was less likely to be spotted by a lunch monitor. The text message read, 63 5th Ave. Naomi F. Preggers?

"What's the assignment?" Avy asked.

"Catch Naomi Fine with a baby bump," I said, and, because Nasim was seriously celebrity challenged, I added, "Big TV star. She plays Cassandra on *Single and Loose*."

Nasim nodded, although I had a feeling he had no idea what *Single and Loose* was. I turned back to Avy. "Is she married?"

Avy, the school's numero uno celebrity media slut, shook his head. "She's dating that high-end Italian hairdresser? Marco with no last name? He used to go out with Ashley Olsen. Only . . . I thought I read that Naomi was shooting a movie in Toronto."

I started to get up, pulling a tattered copy of the school directory out of my bag and dropping it on the table. "Do me a favor? See if anyone at school lives at sixty-three Fifth."

While Avy checked the directory, I headed for the washroom. Cell phone use is supposed to be against the rules, but in private school we're taught to be discreet about breaking them (rules, not cell phones). I locked myself in a stall and called Carla back.

"Nice spread in *New York Weekly,* my dear," she said in a voice made gravelly by years of smoking.

"More like totally amazing, right?" I said. "Just imagine, your client goes from teen newshound to teen newsmaker."

"Don't get a swelled head," my agent cautioned. "What goes up always comes down."

That wasn't exactly what I wanted to hear, but Carla's advice was not to be ignored. She was old enough to be my grandmother and had been in the celebrity business forever.

"Word is that Naomi's ob/gyn doc is here in the city," she said. "My source says she was displaying morning-sickness-like symptoms on the Toronto movie set."

"We know who the doctor is?" I asked.

Carla sighed. "If only, sweetcakes. Wouldn't that make life easy."

I flipped the phone closed. After school, I would have to join the usual cast of scruffy photogs and videographers who were no doubt already hanging around outside 63 Fifth hoping to get a lucky shot of Naomi losing her lunch on the sidewalk. But I didn't have to wait until then to start working the assignment. I had other resources at my disposal.

"Bingo." Avy was pressing his finger down in the school directory when I got back to the dining room.

"You found someone?" I asked excitedly.

"A fifth grader named Ethan Taylor."

We located him sitting with a bunch of boys, collars unbuttoned, ties askew, shirttails hanging half out. Ethan had thick blond hair and a cute upturned nose that belied a long ancestry of lockjawed, God-fearing, WASP bankers.

"Can I talk to you for a second?" I said. "In private."

The other boys began to grin nervously, but Ethan met my gaze calmly. A cool character.

"Go on," one of his friends urged. "See what she wants."

Ethan pushed his chair back, and we walked toward some windows that faced out at a small courtyard garden marked with a plaque that read GIFT OF THE ROCKEFELLER FAMILY.

"You know who Naomi Fine is?" Avy asked. He always got a charge out of being on the case.

Ethan shook his head.

"An actress who lives in your building," I said. "Possibly the penthouse."

"She's on *Single and Loose,* a TV show you're probably not allowed to watch," Avy said.

"You may have seen her with a tall, thin guy who wears his hair in a ponytail?" I added.

Ethan blinked with astonishment. "Oh, yeah. I know who she is!"

"Want to make a hundred dollars?" I asked.

Ethan's eyes widened briefly, then narrowed suspiciously. "You're the one who takes pictures of famous people, right?"

"Help me get the picture I need, and if it gets printed in a magazine or online, it's worth a C-note."

"How?"

"That actress is in the city for a couple of days to see a doctor," I said. "I need to find out who that doctor is. Ask around your building, okay? Chat up the doormen and elevator guys. See what you can learn."

"Why can't I ask my mom?" Ethan asked.

"It would be better if she doesn't know," I said. "She may not be too happy about you making money this way."

"She won't care," Ethan said. "And she's a doctor, too. Actually, I think maybe that Naomi actress could be one of her patients. I remember her once saying she had a really famous patient in the building."

Avy and I exchanged a surprised glance. It sounded too good to be true. "There could be more than one famous person in your building. So you better check it out. Only, this is just between you and me, right?"

"Gotcha." Ethan turned toward the table where his friends sat.

ON THE SCREEN OF YOUR MACBOOK, AVY WILL ASK HIMSELF, "What got you started acting?"

Then, in the role of interviewee, he will reply, "We did a lot of plays and musicals in school, and I discovered that I felt different when I was on stage. Like, more fulfilled, you know? I liked knowing that everyone was watching me. It wasn't like some actors who have to be the center of attention all the time. But when I was in the spotlight I definitely got off on the idea that everyone in the audience knew who I was. And let's face it—I was good at it. People started to say that it seemed like I was born to be on stage. Like I innately knew what to do up there, how to deliver lines, how to project, and where to stand. I had stage presence. Some people get lost on a stage. You hardly know that they're there. Not me. When I was on that stage, everyone knew it."

Your insides will convulse and your heart will twist. Tears will start to run down your cheeks and drip onto the keys of the MacBook. That part is so true. Avy *was* good on the stage. He was funny and full of energy, and he really did seem larger than life. It would be impossible to count the number of times you told him he was the most talented person you knew and how sure you were that he could have a fantastic future as an actor. You believed every word you said. And he believed it, too. Avy Tennent was going to be famous. He was going to be a star.

Next, he will ask, "It's a big leap from school performances to an actual career. How did you prepare for it?"

And he will answer, "I took acting and voice lessons. I went to the acting and modeling conventions and cut school to go to open auditions. That's where the agents saw me, and that's how I signed with Elaine Mazur, my first agent. That really helped, because she could schedule me for auditions after school."

And then he will ask, "How did your parents feel about what you were doing?"

And he will answer, "Truthfully? They weren't paying attention. Elaine would give me papers for them to sign, and I'd forge their signatures. My parents opened a bank account for me when I was fourteen, and I had my own debit card, so when I started getting checks for commercial work I'd deposit them and then use the card to get the money. Elaine's bookkeeper filed my taxes. Everything got sent to our address at home, but my parents almost always worked late, so I'd get to the mailbox first, take out the things for me, and leave the rest of the mail for them. All my parents knew was that I'd done some commercials, and they thought I was going to a few auditions a month. They had no idea I was out there hustling almost every day."

"But they must have found out at some point, right?"

On the screen Avy will say, "Oh, yeah. It all came to a head when I got offered the spot on *Rich and Poor*. The teen reality show, you know? It would have meant being out of school for April and May of freshman year, but the producers promised to hire tutors to help the kids keep up with their schoolwork. You know that kid Brad Cox? The one who's now starring on Nickelodeon's *Dave in Deep*? He got his start on *Rich and Poor* the same season I was supposed to be on the show. And now he's one of the hottest teen stars on TV. That's how close I came. That would have been me."

He will pause here, his face tightening with anger at the memory, and light a cigarette, snapping the Zippo closed. "Of course, there was no way I could miss two months of school without my parents knowing, so I had to talk to them. I tried to reason with them, but that didn't work. Then I begged, I cried, I screamed, I slammed doors. I mean, this went on for days. They just didn't understand. Their son, an actor? No freaking way. Their son, a TV reality show actor? Even worse! Like most stuck-up snobs, they just assumed reality TV was crap. How in the world would that help me get into a good college? What about the so-called career they envisioned for me? You have to understand who my parents are. Typical upwardly mobile, social-climbing uptight white corporate straight arrows. Both lawyers. The types who truly believe that the first eighteen years of life are nothing more than a prelude to a college application."

His hands will be fists, eyes narrowed, jaw jutting forward. For Avy, his parents stopping him from being on the show was the ultimate act of betrayal. It didn't matter that there is no real way to know what would have happened had they let him take the part. For every Brad Cox who goes on to a successful career in TV, there have been hundreds, maybe by this point even thousands, of eager, starstruck wanna-bes whose brief bursts of fame on reality TV shows led nowhere.

"How did you feel about that?" he will ask himself on the screen.

Avy will sit back, cross his arms, and lower his forehead. "You want to know the truth? I've never forgiven them. I hate them."

WHEN I SUGGEST THE SHOT I WANT FOR MY PRIVATE COLLECTION, Rex's face goes stony.

"Oh, come on, Rex, you looked so cute," I beseech him. "I told you it's just for my private collection. I'm already sworn to secrecy about you being here."

But Rex doesn't hear me. He's gone to a different place entirely. He stares at the camera and cringes as if it's bad ju-ju. "Damn, *damn, damn!*"

"What?" I ask, wondering what's suddenly bothering him so much.

He doesn't answer. Instead he runs his fingers through his hair again. Maria slides a mug of steaming coffee in front of him. He takes a sip and looks off toward the glimmering surface of the pool. I wait uncertainly.

"God, I hate this place," he grumbles.

I can't get a grip on what he's talking about or why his mood has shifted so abruptly. "This house?"

He shakes his head, and the long ends of his hair wave against his jawline. "This whole stupid town. This whole stupid scene. Sometimes I wish I'd just stayed in Kilgore."

"But then you . . . you wouldn't have become famous."

Rex's facial expression morphs from puzzlement . . . to recognition . . . to derision. He stares at the camera again, then reaches into his back pocket and pulls out a thin wallet, counts out four Franklins, a Grant, and a bunch of twenties. "How about you sell it to me?"

"My camera? Why?" This makes no sense.

"I don't know. Just feel like taking a few shots myself today."

"Rex, what are you talking about? What's going on?"

Mr. Dobro is experienced in the multiple uses of silence. He stares out at the pool, and once again it's obvious his thoughts are light years away. Or, he just wants me to think that. He takes another sip of coffee and sets the mug down on the counter with a *clink* loud enough that Maria turns to look at him.

He places a hand on my shoulder, and I can't help but think, *Oh my God, he's touching me! Rex Dobro is touching me!* "Don't go anywhere, okay?" he says. "I'll be right back." He pushes away from the counter and leaves the kitchen. I give Maria a puzzled look, but she just shrugs. And why not? She's probably witnessed far stranger things.

But I'm left to wonder what that scene with Rex was all about. I pick up the camera, turn the viewer on, and begin to peruse the previous day's shots. Willow holding the red Manolos she bought me for the party. Willow hanging out by the pool with her best friend, Anne-Marie. Willow and Anne-Marie trying on clothes for the party. I get to the last shot I remember taking the night before—Willow in a slinky pink dress by the pool, welcoming guests. But the camera's counter indicates that there are six more shots. *How weird is this?* I think. First I wake up and my camera isn't where I'm certain I left it. And now I discover I took pictures I don't remember taking.

I flip to the first one . . . and freeze. I am staring at a shot I definitely don't remember taking. And for good reason. I didn't take it.

But that hardly matters now. I've stopped breathing. My heart is thudding. Goose bumps race up my arms, and it might be my imagination, but I think I can feel tiny beads of cold sweat seep out of my pores.

In my camera is a shot that changes everything.

AFTER SCHOOL I WENT STRAIGHT TO THE STAKEOUT AT 63 FIFTH.
Heaven forbid Naomi Fine strolled out the front doors
looking like a whale and I wasn't there to get the shot.
Carla would have my head.

"The baby's here!" a videographer named David Axelrod
yelled when I arrived. About a dozen photogs were hanging
around in front of the tall brick building. Davy was one of
the nicer ones. There were others in that crowd who would
break your face if you got in the way of one of their shots.

"Go home and do your homework," Davy said in a
good-natured jibe. "Leave this business to people who
really need to make a living."

A woman named Lynn who always wore a khaki vest and had two or three cameras hanging from her neck strolled over and took a rapid-fire series of shots of Davy and me.

"What's this about?" Davy asked her.

"Didn't you see that article in *New York Weekly*?" Lynn asked, then pointed at me. "She's news. The baby paparazzo. I want these for my files."

She went back to the others waiting on the sidewalk for Naomi to appear. But for me it was an oddly strange and gratifying moment to be on the other side of the camera—continued evidence that I was *still* news. My fifteen minutes weren't over yet.

"How's it feel to be famous?" Davy asked, only half-kidding.

I knew that he was partly teasing. And yet the idea that I might be famous—just the *possibility* of it—felt undeniably satisfying. "Better than not being famous."

"So, what's your next move?"

That caught me off guard. "Sorry?"

"The next step," Davy said. "You're not gonna drop the ball now, are you? You've got some recognition. Momentum. That gives you a window of what? A month? Maybe two? After that, people are gonna forget who you are, and you'll go back to being just another paparazzo."

It wasn't something I'd thought about. The whole idea

of being famous was still too new for me to be concerned about the possibility of it vanishing. "I'll let you know."

"Hey, here's something else." Davy opened a copy of *Teen Seen,* a sort of cheap *Cosmo* for the training-bra set, and showed me a photo of a gorgeous young woman with straight black hair and striking features. "The future."

I read the caption. "Alicia Howard?"

"My eleven-year-old niece says she's the real deal," Davy said. "The next Willow Twine."

"Don't tell Willow that," I quipped.

Davy shook his head dismissively. "Willow's on her way out. Once you start running with guys like Rex Dobro, it's only a matter of time."

"You can't say that for certain. She might be an exception."

Davy gave me a dubious look. "Sorry, kid, they lose that sheen of girlish innocence and *poof!* The glass slipper never fits again."

Shutters began clicking rapidly, and Davy and I spun around. Marco was coming down the sidewalk. He was tall and skinny, wore tight black leather pants, and had his hair pulled back into a ponytail. With those lanky legs he took long strides, making it hard for the crowd of photogs to keep up with him and still frame their shots.

"Over here, Marco!"

"Hey, Marco, this way!"

"Is Naomi pregnant?"

"When's she due?"

"Is it a boy or a girl, Marco?"

The famous hairdresser ignored them and kept walking. It was the smartest thing he could do, but it was also exactly what some of the more aggressive paps wanted.

"So how's it feel to be a father, Marco?"

"You gonna do the right thing and tie the knot?"

"Or are you gonna dump her as soon as she gets fat?"

"Hey, Marco, you sure the kid's even yours?"

Ouch!

It was then that Marco went from smart to stupid. He did two of the three worst things you can do when in the paparrazzi's sights: (1) He stopped, and (2) he reacted. Once you stop, you're surrounded. The photogs move in shoulder to shoulder and make it hard for you to start moving again. And I don't have to tell you why reacting is a mistake. Look at any tabloid or celebrity website and you can see for yourself.

Marco started growling in English and Italian, and the clicking shutters around him hit that crescendo that screams *Money Shot!* Most of what Marco said in English was unprintable, and the photogs loved it.

"Looks like we hit a sore spot, huh, Marco?"

"Yeah, just where *was* Naomi about three months ago?"

"Hey, wasn't she shooting that rodeo movie out in Montana with Anthony Impalino?"

"Maybe she's having Tony junior!"

Marco's eyes bulged and his hands balled into fists. It looked like he was on the verge of making the numero uno biggest mistake of all. One that would cost him big-time. The more brazen photogs moved in closer and kept shooting, mostly for the annoyance factor. I could feel my heart banging in anticipation. Would Marco take the bait and swing at one of them? Didn't he know he could be sued for millions?

Yes, it appeared he did. At the very last second he seemed to get a grip on himself, then slid through the crowd of photographers and strode through the doors and into the building, where none of us could follow.

Ready . . . set . . . go!

Photogs scattered in every direction to get to their cars, studios, apartments—wherever they could download their shots and videos into laptops and transmit them to agents and websites. For me, that meant running down Fifth Avenue and making a right on Eleventh Street.

At home Elena was spooning Alex dinner. My brother wears a bib. The soft foods protect him from choking, but they also drip off his chin and onto the bib despite Elena's best efforts to wipe them away. Alex saw me and made sounds as I flew into the apartment. "Hey, Elena. Hey, Axy Waxy," I called as I passed. Usually, when I wasn't in a rush, I'd rub my brother's head. He has the finest, softest hair you've ever felt. A long time ago the specialists told us physical contact was really important. But right then I had to get on the computer fast, download my shots, and blast them off through broadband to Carla. Strapped in his chair, Alex lurched and grimaced and made deeper grunting sounds. It was his way of saying he was unhappy that I hadn't paused to greet him properly.

In my room I downloaded my shots onto the MacBook, narrowed the selection to a few dozen, and sent them to Carla. I'd already called her from the street and alerted her that I had the goods: Marco nearly pitching a fit. (While I personally didn't go in for the stalkerazzi technique of taunting and harassing, I wasn't above reaping the benefits.)

I doubt half a minute passed between the time I e-mailed the photos and when Carla called. "You did good, girl. I've definitely got clients who'll want these. We may even sell enough to get you that long lens you want. Later." She was gone. There were editors to call, deals to make. I logged in to the private client website where she displayed all the photos she had for sale. To prevent anyone from stealing the photos without paying, the agents all had computer programs designed to make our shots look lo-res blurry and grainy, and the word COPYRIGHTED was printed across them, obscuring key details.

It was too soon for the celebrity websites to have the videographers' stuff up—their raw footage would have to be edited first—but I checked anyway, always curious to see if I'd show up in the crowd of photogs in the background. When you're a pap you're on TV and in magazines all the time, only no one ever notices, because they're always too busy looking at the celebs.

Since the videos weren't up yet, I got on Facebook. Nasim was on, so we shot some IMs back and forth.

Jamie Gordan Got some good shots of Naomi's boyfriend freaking out.

Nasim Pahlavi What about the pregnant actress?

Jamie Gordan No sign of her.

Nasim Pahlavi So instead you use the boyfriend to make up for the photos you couldn't get?

Jamie Gordan Try not to be so perceptive, okay? ;-)

Nasim Pahlavi I thought that's what you like about me ;-)

Jamie Gordan It is!!! So . . . what do you like about me?

Nasim didn't answer right away, and I felt my spirits start to sink. Sometimes it seemed like there was something missing from our relationship. Like on some level we weren't as intimate as we should have been. I told myself that maybe it was just a cultural thing, that Nasim wasn't used to expressing his feelings out loud. But I wasn't sure. I waited a while, then began to feel a little bit anxious, so I wrote:

Jamie Gordan I hope your silence means there are

so many things you like about me that you don't know where to begin ;-0 ???

Nasim Pahlavi Try not to be so perceptive, okay? ;-)

Jamie Gordan LOL.

Nasim Pahlavi I like that you are caring and honest and don't worry so much about things like grades (which proves that for us opposites attract) or popularity. I like that you are pretty and soft and smart.

Jamie Gordan Thank you! XOXOX!

I loved what he wrote, even though I had a feeling that "soft" was just a really sweet way of saying I could lose ten pounds.

Elena knocked on my door. "Alex is watching TV. Not alone too long, okay?"

"You bet," I said, and looked back at the screen.

In the time I'd been turned away, a new IM had come on the screen.

Shelby Winston Having some people over on Sat night around 10. Hope you can join us. Bring the BF.—SW

"Thanks for agreeing to go to the party with me," I said to Nasim the next morning as we walked to school through a slight gray mist. It was the sort of gauzy light that had posed interesting possibilities to me back when I'd been taking more "artistic" pictures.

"You already thanked me last night," he said. As soon as I'd seen the invitation I'd IM'd him, and he'd agreed to go. But now I wondered if maybe he wasn't thrilled by the idea.

"You think it's dumb, right?" I asked.

"To be excited about going to a party? Why would that be dumb?"

"Because it's Shelby Winston's party."

"Wouldn't you be as excited if it were Avy's party?" he asked.

"Honestly? Not really. I mean, I'd be happy that he invited me and happy to go, but I can't say I'd be as excited."

Nasim put his arm around my shoulder and gave me a squeeze. "If it's important to you, then it's important to me."

I slid my arm under his jacket and around his waist, thinking that one could hardly ask for a better boyfriend, and about how lucky I was.

By then we'd passed through the front doors and entered the hallowed halls of Herrin. It didn't occur to me that the blond-haired kid blocking my path actually wanted to talk to me. I started to walk around him.

Nasim took my arm. "Wait. It's your fifth-grade spy."

Ethan Taylor handed me a piece of paper with a name and address written on it. Then he rubbed his thumb against his fingers—the universal "Show me the money" gesture.

"You get paid when I get paid," I said in a low voice, folding the piece of paper and sliding it into my pocket. I glanced back down the hall at the school entrance and started to zip my jacket.

"Where are you going?" Nasim asked with a frown.

"To the doctor's," I said.

It's the strangest sensation when you're the only photog on a stakeout. It felt like there'd been a mistake and that Ethan must have gotten it wrong. I was standing on a sidewalk beside a tall sand-colored building. But the doctor's office had its own entrance—a black door a dozen feet from the building's main entrance—and a well-polished bronze plate next to the door said very clearly,

DR. EMILY CLARKSON

OBSTETRICS AND GYNECOLOGY

A woman wearing a fur-lined raincoat passed, walking a pug wearing its own bright red raincoat. The street was filled with cars and yellow taxis, wipers swishing the mist off their windshields.

For better or worse I was committed to this plan. The damage was done. I'd left school without permission and was bound to get grief for it. All I could do was wait and hope this gamble paid off. Women carrying umbrellas came down the sidewalk and went into the office. Cabs pulled up to the curb and dropped people off. After about an hour a limo slid up, and the driver ran around to the passenger door. My heart started to race. Was it Naomi? But out stepped an elegant older woman wearing a Burberry taffeta trench coat and a hat. False alarm.

I waited in the mist, my hair practically soaked. Lunch time came and went. My stomach growled and my feet throbbed from standing so long, but I couldn't give up now. What if I left and Naomi showed up a minute later? Another hour passed. More women came and went. At the building's main entrance, a doorman wearing a brown uniform noticed me and scowled, but I hid my camera under my jacket so he wouldn't know why I was there.

The longer I waited, the more doubts plagued me. Maybe Ethan was right about the address and doctor, but Naomi's appointment was yesterday and I'd missed it. Or maybe it wasn't until tomorrow. Was this worth ditching another day of school for? How much trouble would I get into?

And then, in the middle of all my dithering, a cab pulled up and out stepped Naomi Fine wearing a baseball cap and an open zip-front hoodie, her hair pulled back in a ponytail. She wore a jumper under the hoodie, and maybe that was or wasn't a baby bump, but her breasts looked large and full, and something about her face shouted "Flush of motherhood!"

Knowing instinctively I'd have to make it a profile shot because there wasn't enough baby bump to see from the front, I took out my camera and started to shoot. I could tell this was something Naomi Fine could not have expected, because she was wearing that hat and plain clothes. After all, she was supposed to be on location in Toronto, and there should have been no way a stranger would have recognized her, right? She actually stopped on the sidewalk and gave me an absolutely classic look of utter astonishment.

And there it was—the money shot.

Less than a minute later I was in a cab headed to Carla's office because this shot was big, Big, *BIG*! and I was totally freaked that something terrible might happen before I could get the photo to her—like the camera might unexpectedly die or an earthquake might hit New York, or the entire solar system might be swallowed by a black hole—but none of those things happened, and Carla was waiting outside her office for me with an umbrella because I'd called ahead and told her what I had.

Carla was more ageless than old. My best guess was that she was between sixty-five and seventy-five, but you'd never know it from the way she acted. She was short and plump and had enough energy to keep a small city lit for months. As soon as I got out of the cab we raced up to her office like two giddy kids who'd just gotten their hands on a big bag of candy, and I watched over her shoulder, my nostrils filled with the mixed scents of Chanel N°5 and stale cigarettes, while she transferred the shots onto her Mac Pro. I felt instantly and totally relieved, because now even an earthquake couldn't stop us, and Carla scrolled down to the money shot and let out a scream and jumped up and hugged me and we both danced around the office like crazy people.

And then she was on the phone to the top editors because this shot was so hot she didn't even dare put it in lo res on her private website.

And the bidding began.

By the time I left her office two hours later, we'd sold my first cover shot to *People* magazine.

And my first year of college was probably paid for.

Although, honestly, I was seriously wondering, why bother with college?

It was dinnertime when I sailed into the kitchen. Mom was on the phone, still wearing her work clothes. I waved my hands excitedly, gesturing for her to get off so I could tell her the news. The expression on her face was icy. "She just walked in," she said into the receiver. "I'll speak to her. Thank you."

"Mom," I began to say, "you won't believe—"

"That was Mrs. Krohn, the school secretary," Mom sharply cut me off. "Where were you today?"

"Well, uh, I was at school for a second," I said. "But I had to leave."

Mom cocked her head and raised an eyebrow, silently demanding an explanation. I was happy to provide it.

"Because I got some information about Naomi Fine? The actress? The whole world wants to know if she's pregnant and I—"

"You cut school to go take pictures?" Mom asked, emphasizing the incredulity in her voice so I'd know how PO'd she was.

"Yes, but—"

Mom shook her head, as if she wasn't interested in my explanations. "What do I have to do?" She tilted her face upward and raised her hands in exasperation as if pleading with a higher being. "Tell me, Jamie. What *do* I have to do? Do I have to take away the camera? Ground you? I'm tired of this stupid game you're playing. You're *not* a paparazzo. You're a young woman who happened to get lucky once. And then that stupid magazine decided to make a spectacle of you because you're so young. And now you're living in this fantasy world where you actually think you're a professional. It's as if you're still playing with dolls, Jamie. You're *not* a photographer. You're just a little girl with a camera. Can't you understand the difference?"

The kitchen went silent. I knew I could have gotten mad. I could have yelled back. But in a strange way, I understood where she was coming from, and I wasn't mad. Everything she said was true. It *was* strange and unreal. I *was* just a kid with a camera. That's exactly what I felt like. And yet . . .

I took out my cell phone, dialed Carla's number, and held it out toward my mother.

"What are you doing?" Mom asked with a frown.

"I want you to speak to Carla."

Mom stared at the phone and shook her head. "I have nothing to say to that woman. She should be ashamed of herself. All she's doing is perpetuating this fantasy."

I was still holding the phone, but I had not yet pressed send. "You don't want to know how much money I made today? You don't want to hear that I just sold a cover to *People*?"

My mother's forehead furrowed as she looked at me uncertainly. I guess she was realizing that either I was telling the truth or had gone really, truly, certifiably insane. Finally she said, "Are you serious?"

I nodded at the phone. "Ask Carla."

Mom shook her head and sat down wearily at the kitchen table. "I don't want to talk to that woman. I'm tired of playing games. Put the phone away and tell me what happened."

I sat down and told her how I had staked out Dr. Emily Clarkson's office until Naomi Fine arrived.

"How did you know she'd show up?" Mom asked.

"She's in the middle of a movie shoot in Toronto," I said. "It costs hundreds of thousands a day to shoot a movie. They don't give stars days off, so if Naomi came to New York to see her doctor it meant it must have been a really pressing issue. She took a private jet. It made sense that if she was pregnant, she'd have to get to the doctor fast and then fly back."

Mom stared at me in wonder.

"Mom, it's not rocket surgery. It's obvious. Everybody assumed that she was pregnant. It's just that I was the only one who figured out who her doctor was."

Then I told her how much money *People* had agreed to pay for the shot. Mom's jaw dropped. She looked as if she'd lost her breath. Even though she thought the celebrity magazines and TV shows and tabloids and websites and the whole American obsession with celebrity in general were completely loony, she understood how big this was.

"And you know what's really whacked, Mom?" I said. "You're completely right. I *am* just a girl with a camera. And I *am* living in a fantasy world. But the crazy thing is, so is everyone else."

That night I lay awake in bed, way too excited to sleep, my thoughts racing. I was about to win the equivalent of Olympic Gold for paparazzi—a *People* cover! It was amazing and unreal, and I both knew and didn't know what I'd done to deserve it. I didn't blame my mother for having doubted me. Looking back, it was incredibly lucky that I went to the same school as Ethan Taylor, whose mother was Naomi Fine's eye doctor.

(And yes, he sure did get his one hundred dollars.) But I also believe that luck doesn't just happen. You have to create opportunities for it. I didn't have to get my camera ready when I sensed something might happen with Tatiana Frazee in Cafazine. I didn't have to track Ethan down. I didn't have to gamble on ditching a day of school to hang around outside Dr. Clarkson's office. And the other thing is, no one wants to hear about all the times I stood around on stakeouts for hours but got nothing for my efforts except sore feet and a head cold. That's where persistence eventually pays off. If you keep trying and trying, sooner or later you'll probably get lucky. Like the Lottery ad says, "You've got to be in it to win it."

That Saturday Nasim's parents went to the opera, and he made me a traditional Persian dinner of naan, yogurt, lamb, and vegetable kebabs with rice. We ate by candlelight in the Pahlavis' formal dining room, an ancient tapestry of a princess and a unicorn hanging on the wall beside us.

We talked about school and friends, but it wasn't long before the subject turned to my forthcoming *People* cover. The truth was, it was difficult for me to think about anything else.

"How do you do it?" he asked.

"I told you," I said. "I just stood there and waited, hoping she'd show up."

"No, what I meant was, how do you know when to take the picture? How do you know whether it's a good picture or not?"

"I don't always know," I said. "That's why I shoot rapid-fire."

"I remember when we first met, before you were shooting celebrities, you would take a long time to set up just one photo."

Was it my imagination, or did I detect something subtly critical in his words? Was he implying that the photos I used to take were more artistic and therefore somehow better? "I'm not doing that kind of photography these days."

He nodded, took a sip of water, then dabbed his lips with a cloth napkin. We'd finished dinner.

"Does it bother you that I don't take the kind of photos I used to take?" I asked a little bit later while he rinsed the dishes in the kitchen and loaded them into the dishwasher.

"No," he said. "But must it be one or the other? Can't you do a little of both?"

"I guess I could, but that's not what I want to do right now."

Nasim dried his hands with a dishtowel. "Want to watch the movie?"

"Okay." I'd brought over *Persepolis,* the animated movie about a rebellious girl growing up in Iran. I still couldn't shake the feeling that Nasim disapproved of the pictures I was taking. But I didn't want to spoil the mood and decided to drop it.

We went into the living room and sat on the couch. Nasim's arm was over my shoulder and I nestled my head against his neck. I thought he'd pick up the remote and start the movie, but instead he brushed some hair away from my face, leaned over, and kissed me. "I'm proud of what you do."

"You sure?" I asked uncertainly.

"Yes."

"Well then, thank you," I said, and kissed him back.

It started to look like we might not get around to watching the movie. I tried to forget our discussion about my photography and lose myself in the moment, but I didn't succeed completely. Then the alarm on my cell phone chimed. I gradually eased out of Nasim's embrace and turned it off. "I can't believe it's time already," I mumbled, straightening my clothes.

"Sorry?" Nasim's brow furrowed.

"Shelby's party."

His dark eyebrows dipped. I could tell that he'd forgotten about the party and had other ideas about how to spend the next few hours. "Are you sure?" he asked.

I didn't want to disappoint him, but I just had to go to that party. "You know how much this means to me." I gave him a kiss on the cheek and stood up. Nasim still hadn't moved from the couch, so I grabbed his hand and gave him a tug. "Come on, we'll have fun."

I knew Nasim wasn't happy about going to the party, and on the way over I tried to explain to him that it wasn't like I was choosing the party over him. It was just a matter of timing. He said he understood, but once again I got that feeling that deep down he wasn't allowing me to see his true feelings. It was frustrating, but I'd learned from experience that there was nothing I could do about it.

It turned out that the party wasn't as much fun as I'd hoped. Shelby's little get-together turned out to be a catered affair for 120 people in a rented loft in Soho. Most of the kids weren't from Herrin, and Shelby was so busy introducing me to everyone as "the one from the *New York Weekly* article," that we never actually got a chance to speak.

Each time she mentioned the article, I had to bite my lip to keep myself from telling her about the *People* cover, but I was terrified that would jinx the whole thing. Nasim, who'd been a little grumpy ever since we'd left his place, tagged along for a while but finally wandered away after he'd heard me answer the same questions for the tenth time. At one point I saw him talking to Shelby and felt jealous that he was getting more face time with her than I was.

My mother and Nasim were the only ones who knew about the *People* cover, and I made them swear not to tell a soul. I didn't even tell Avy or my father. I was convinced that the more people who knew, the greater the chance that the whole thing would be jinxed—that an even bigger story would break and the editors at *People* would pick a different cover photo, or that Naomi would get a restraining order to stop the magazine from publishing my shot.

After all, it really was too good to be true, wasn't it? First the Tatiana Frazee shots, then the *New York Weekly* story, and now the *People* cover? That was *way* too much good fortune. Something *had* to go wrong, didn't it?

But nothing did. Five days later *People* hit the newsstands with my photo of the pregnant Naomi Fine. By third period, copies of the magazine were flying around school, along with the whispers and the stares.

"This is ab-so-lutely amazing!" Avy gushed at lunch, a copy of *People* lying on the table before us. "Now you're going to be even more famous!"

I wondered if he was right, and what exactly "more famous" would mean. But maybe it wouldn't happen. "Not really," I said. "Unless you know where to look and have a magnifying glass, most people aren't going to notice my photo credit."

"But you got paid a ton, right?" Avy said.

I nodded.

"And it is good for your reputation," added the ever

insightful Nasim with a tinge of irony in his voice.

"True, all that," I said, and glanced toward the table where Shelby Winston was sitting with her friends. Shelby gazed back at me with a smile and lifted a copy of the magazine. She pointed at the cover, made an OMG! face, and winked.

My star was definitely on the rise.

NEW YORK PRESS
Baby Pap Scoops the Pros Again!

Jamie Gordon, the "baby paparazzo" has done it again! The fifteen-year-old prodigy photographer, featured three weeks ago in a *New York Weekly* magazine profile, has nailed the cover of *People* with a shot confirming that actress Naomi Fine is pregnant. Photo editors and fellow photographers are agog.

"First the Tatiana Frazee child-abuse shots," quipped one editor. "Now the Naomi Fine baby bump. It's amazing. Either this kid is the luckiest thing ever, or she really knows what she's doing."

"It would be a remarkable accomplishment for any paparazzo," agreed another. "But for a kid that age, it's mind-boggling."

Some of Jamie's fellow photographers are understandably jealous. "I'm not impressed," said one. "Some people are saying that the first time might have been luck, but the second means she's for real. But lots of people get lucky twice. They even hit the Lottery twice. Let's see how long it takes for her to scoop everyone again."

The newspaper article featured a side-by-side display of the *People* cover and a photo of me taken by that paparazzo, Lynn, outside Naomi Fine's building the day Marco the hairdresser freaked out. And, just as Avy had predicted, that was only the beginning. The story was picked up by national TV and dozens of other news outlets. Suddenly I knew what "more famous" meant. I was interviewed and photographed, TV news teams followed me from school to my stakeouts with other photogs. At one stakeout outside a restaurant, Seth Rogen made a joke out of coming up to me and asking for *my* autograph!

Dad and I flew to LA for the *Tonight Show*. Even though I barely slept on the red-eye coming home, I went straight to Herrin from the airport the next morning, running on adrenaline and doing my best not to miss more school and tick my mother off. And, of course, looking forward to basking in everyone's admiration.

After all, there I was on TV, the Web, the supermarket news racks. For the moment I was not just the most well-known high school student in New York.

I was, quite possibly, one of the best-known high school students in the country.

If not the world.

After school I trudged home, pulling my roller suitcase stuffed with outfits I'd brought for the *Tonight Show*. I was toast, completely exhausted after catching at most only two or three hours of sleep on the plane the night before. I left the suitcase in the front hall and went into the kitchen. Mom was sitting at the kitchen table, staring down at a mug of tea cupped in her hands, looking haggard and pale. I knew at once that something was wrong.

"What happened?" I asked.

She looked up at me with red-rimmed eyes. "Alex had a seizure. Elena was taking him for a walk. Luckily they weren't far from St. Vincent's."

"Is he okay?" I asked.

"Yes, thank God. It wasn't a bad one. We just got home half an hour ago. He's in his room, resting. But it was terrible. I was so scared when I got that call. I had to cancel all my afternoon appointments and rush down there. My patients know about Alex, and they say they understand when I have to cancel at the last minute. But not everyone reschedules. Each time something like this happens, I lose patients. . . . Sometimes"—her voice cracked—"I just don't know if I can handle it."

She placed a hand over her eyes and began to weep. Her shoulders trembled, and she looked old and drawn. She wasn't just crying because she was tired and scared; she was crying because it was so unfair.

"Can't Dad help?" I asked. "Couldn't Alex stay with him more?"

"It's not practical." Mom pulled the tears from the

corners of her eyes with her fingertips. "Alex needs so much medical equipment. The insurance company won't pay for duplicates just because we're divorced. And anyway, I'm always worried something will happen when he's at your father's place."

"Even though you know what you know?" I asked.

Mom raised her head, wiped her reddened eyes with the back of her hand, and scowled at me. The tic around her left eye came back. It took her a moment to understand what I'd meant. Nearly everyone with muscular dystrophy dies by the time they reach twenty-five. "Don't say that. Medicine is constantly making advances."

That was, of course, true. But it had been more than a hundred years since muscular dystrophy was first identified, and people diagnosed with it today still didn't live much longer with it than they did a century ago.

Mom was quiet for a moment, and I knew she was listening for any sounds coming from Alex's room. Then she stood up, kissed the top of my head, and left the kitchen as if she were on autopilot. She would check on Alex, take care of whatever business still demanded her attention from earlier in the day, try to figure out what to do about dinner, let Elena go home, take care of Alex for the rest of the evening, and then collapse into bed, only to start the whole process over again tomorrow.

It would have been totally selfish to feel upset that she'd completely blanked on the fact that just seven hours ago I'd landed at JFK on my way back from a TV taping in LA. Way too much had happened with Alex during that time, and she had way too much on her mind.

And yet, I couldn't help feeling bad.

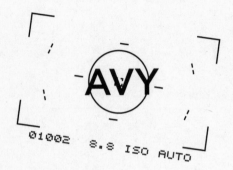

I WOULDN'T BE SITTING ON THIS DUMB TROLLEY RIGHT now, shivering in the AC with wads of drug money taped around my stomach, if it weren't for my parents. Instead I'd probably still be in New York, just where they want me to be. But they were so stupid. This is what you get when you can't compromise.

I had a huge opportunity with *Rich and Poor,* and Mom and Dad just arbitrarily snuffed it. Can you blame me if I totally hate them? They kept saying, "We're doing this for your own good. Someday you'll understand." Well, the only thing I understand is that the only people they care about is themselves. It wasn't like I wanted to join some weird religious cult. I kept telling them that acting is what I'll want to do for the rest of my life. And they were, like, "Oh, you're too young to know what you really want," and "How is acting on a reality TV show going to help you get into a good college?"

College? Hello? Is anyone even freaking listening? Hey, Mom, Dad, how many times have I told you I don't give a crap about college? Do you have any idea how few famous actors went to college? Or went for a year or two and dropped out?

And then one day it hit me. I had a choice. I could either go through life blaming my parents or I could decide the hell with them and move on. It didn't matter what they thought or wanted. They were worried about me not going to a *good* college? How about me not going to any college at all?

That was the moment everything changed. It was almost like I wasn't their son anymore. Like I'd stepped through a portal into a different dimension. I was on my own, and it was up to me to decide what was best for my career.

Thanks to the commercials I'd done, I already had some money in the bank . . . and God bless eBay. In one week I almost doubled my money by selling practically everything I owned. Guitars, Xbox, camera, sneakers, Grampa's wristwatch—you name it, I sold it. Then I went on Craigslist and found a room to rent in a house in North Hollywood.

I bought one-way tickets on the Lake Shore Limited to Chicago and the Southwest Chief from Chicago to LA, left a note on the dining room table, and was out of there for good.

N,
I wish you'd write. I said I was sorry. I promise I'll make it up to you when I get back to New York. I want you to tell me everything there is to know about you. Seriously. Please?

Anyway, here's the latest: Willow's raven-haired friend is Ann-Marie. She's the daughter of some big cable TV mogul and incredibly rich and thin. So is Willow. (You forget that the camera adds ten pounds).

As soon as Ann-Marie arrived, Willow came downstairs and we went out to the pool. A-M and Willow wore bikinis and have amazing bodies (Just between you and me, N, I think they must have had matching boob jobs. Maybe they got a 4 for 2 deal!!!).

I was incredibly self-conscious in my one-piece suit, and A-M wasn't exactly friendly. The first words out of her mouth to me were, "So where's your camera?"

Nice, huh?

At the pool, Willow was constantly on the phone. She had two kinds of conversations:

1. "Yes" conversations (mostly with friends): "Oh, hi . . . Chillaxing by the pool. Oh, yeah? That might be cool. Okay, let me know. Ciao!"

2. "No" conversations (mostly about business): "No, I never said I'd do that. No way! In his dreams! That's why they invented (fill in the blank: stunt people, body doubles, personal assistants, limo drivers, publicists, etc., etc.)."

Is this the secret of Willow's success? Saying no makes people want you more?

BTW--have you heard from Avy? The phone number I have for him doesn't work, and he hasn't answered any of my e-mails. I hope it's because he's really busy. If I don't hear from him soon I'm going to have to go track him down at Starwood, the showbiz-kids condo development where he's staying.

Back to Willow. We hung by the pool for a while, then she decided to try on some of the things she bought that day. She asked me to get my camera and did a little fashion show in her bedroom with Ann-Marie approving or disapproving. Nothing to get excited about. (I'll show you the shots when I get home.)

After the fashion show we went to dinner. There were six of us at a round table in the back of the restaurant. Sam had us sit in a semicircle with Willow in the middle and her back against the wall. The others were Ann-Marie, the two girls from the shopping trip--Kristen and Lanie--and Sam and me.

Willow and her friends picked at their food and gossiped. Now and then someone approached the table for an autograph.

They passed a napkin, autograph book, menu (bet the restaurant really appreciated that), to one of us and we passed it to Willow. She smiled and signed everything.

(Rule #1 for the care and nurturing of stars: Once a day take them somewhere they can sign autographs. It makes them feel good.)

Spent the rest of the day shooting Willow at the beach, at the gym, riding a bike, eating a salad for lunch. See Willow play! See Willow eat! See how healthy and well-adjusted Willow is!

Last night after dinner we piled into a big white SUV and Sam drove us to Glare, the hottest club in LA. The sidewalk was roped off; the line of clubbers stretched down the block. Paparazzi hovered. As soon as we arrived the flashes began. (Once again it's weird to be on the other side of the camera!) Paps shouting, "How do you feel about Rex seeing Dominika Bartoli?"

"How was rehab?"

"Think you can stay drug free?"

Willow was cool under fire. She

smiled for the cameras and ignored the questions. Sam stayed close and hustled us past the line and into the club. (No one checks IDs in LA?)

Thunderous music inside. Willow and her friends joined the dancing crowd. Guys began circling. You could see the word spreading that Willow Twine was there. People leaning to one another and yelling in ears. Heads turning, necks craning for a look.

Willow asked Sam to get her a bottle of water. Get this--she isn't allowed to have anything from an open glass unless Sam pours it himself. I took a bunch of pictures and was headed back toward Sam when someone grabbed my hand. It was Willow; she wanted me to dance.

So, why not? I danced with her and her friends and lost myself in the music and movement. (Don't worry, N, no one hit on me). At one point I was face-to-face with Willow and she kissed me on the cheek! (No, that doesn't count as hitting on me ;-)

Suddenly something in the air changed. All around us lips were pressed to ears, and murmurs rippled through the crowd. A group of lanky guys had come in. Spiked hair, tattoos, and piercings. At the center was Rex Dobro!

N, it was electric! Like an old western movie where the gunfighters face off. Everyone stopped dancing. A camera (not mine) flashed. Sam launched himself through the crowd toward Willow. Suddenly they were gone.

The music was still playing. At first I didn't know what to do, but when Willow's friends started dancing and flirting with guys again, I figured I'd just wait. That's when I noticed that Rex's friends were still there, but not Rex.

After a while Sam came back alone and said he'd drive me home. The other girls all stayed.

On the way back, I asked where Willow was. Sam's answer: "Nowhere good."

Wonder what he meant.

Really miss you. Would love a hit back. xoxoxox?

DETECTIVE
CARLOS
RAMOS

01002   8.8 ISO AUTO

I work for the Threat Management Unit of the Los Angeles Police Department. Some people call it the Celebrity Antistalking Unit. We handle about 250 cases a year.

In my experience, most stalkers are annoying but basically harmless. The problem is, you never know for sure, so you have to approach each one the same way—as if they have the potential to do serious harm.

By the way, I know this has nothing to do with what we're talking about, but you want to know what one of our most annoying problems is? Imaginary stalkers. The ones that don't exist—except in a celebrity's mind.

We've got a couple of those right now. Some celebrity starts thinking, "Hey, I'm famous, and famous people have stalkers, therefore, I must have a stalker." Next thing you know, they start seeing stalkers everywhere.

I'm telling you, live and learn. Work this unit long enough and you'll see everything.

Richard Hildebrandt was what we call a "love obsessional" stalker. At least, that's how he started out. He decided he was in love with Willow Twine. He became obsessed with her. He decided that if he could somehow meet her, she'd recognize his true love and love him back. Only with Hildebrandt, there were bigger issues. Definitely an element of schizophrenia. He believed that there were people who wanted to harm her and that he had to protect her from them.

Only, he was also the one who wanted to harm her. I'm no shrink, but obviously this was one very messed up character.

AS FALL FADED INTO WINTER, THE EXCITEMENT OF ALL MY PUBLICITY ABOUT being the youngest paparazzo seemed to fade with it. My appearance on *The Tonight Show* was forgotten. The issue of *People* with my cover was recycled and mulched with all the other magazines. Naomi Fine grew more pregnant and announced plans to marry Marco. Just as Davy's niece had predicted, Alicia Howard burst onto the scene as the star of the new Nickelodeon series *Garage Girls* (about an all-girl garage band) and released her first CD, which debuted at number seventeen on the charts and quickly shot to number one.

By the time winter blossomed into spring, my career

momentum had wound down to something slower than a crawl, as if, at the age of fifteen, I was already a has-been.

"Wouldn't you rather be a has-been than a never was?" Davy asked one afternoon after I confided to him that whatever social currency I'd earned the previous fall must have fallen through a hole in my pocket.

"I'm fifteen, Davy," I answered indignantly. "Isn't that a little young?"

He shrugged and didn't verbalize what we both knew: Fifteen was plenty old enough to be a has-been. Just ask Macaulay Culkin, the former child superstar of the *Home Alone* movies, or Molly Ringwald, who starred in all those John Hughes movies, like *The Breakfast Club, Pretty in Pink,* and *Sixteen Candles.* My fifteen minutes were over, and it left me feeling slightly empty, as if I'd lost something and didn't know how to get it back. No one whispered or stared at me in school anymore.

Things had pretty much gone back to normal at home, too.

"It would be nice if you spent more time with your brother," Mom said one morning before school while I dumped my camera bag onto the kitchen table and poured myself a cup of coffee.

"I will," I said, taking a sip.

"You always say that," Mom replied.

"Between school and work and Nasim, I'm busy," I said. But the truth was, I wasn't feeling busy because I had *too much* to do, I felt busy because I didn't have *enough*. Months had passed since I'd sold a photo. Carla kept telling me to be patient, but it wasn't easy. I felt like everyone was expecting something from the paparazzo prodigy. In addition to "has-been," phrases like "flash in the pan" and "one-hit wonder" buzzed around my thoughts like annoying gnats. Were all the naysayers right? Was I only a kid with a camera who'd gotten really lucky twice?

By April, yellow and purple crocuses had begun to spring up in Washington Square. There were green buds on the trees, and on warm afternoons people threw Frisbees and hung out around the fountain. I was sitting in Nasim's living room while he sat at the baby grand playing Bartók's *Allegro Barbaro*. Nasim didn't particularly *like* piano, but he played it for the same reason that he worked so hard to have a stellar GPA and flawless manners—because he was supposed to.

With a recital only a week away, he was practicing full run-throughs of the entire fifteen-minute piece. I sat on the broad windowsill, knees tucked under my chin, gazing down at the park, wondering what famous person might be pushing a baby stroller while getting some fresh spring air. I felt antsy; I could have been down there, shooting.

In the middle of that thought my cell phone vibrated. Trying not to be obvious, I checked and saw that it was Carla. I glanced over at Nasim, whose head was bent over the keys, then slid off the windowsill. Nasim immediately glanced up and gave me a look of displeasure, but he continued playing. I went into the kitchen, closed the door, and called her back.

"What's up?" I asked.

"Are you sitting down?" she asked with the nearly breathless excitement that almost always signaled good news. "I just got a call from Roxanne Pena, Alicia Howard's publicist. Alicia's going to be in New York next week to tape the *Late Show*. She also wants to do some shopping and take a break from LA . . . and she wants you to shoot her."

Goose bumps rose on my arms. "Why me?"

"According to Roxanne, Alicia saw you on the *Tonight Show* last fall and decided that you would 'get' her. I think she meant you'd understand her. You know, because you're around the same age."

"They want me to shadow her?" I asked.

"Not quite. They'll set up the times and places. You know the drill. 'See Alicia shop. See Alicia at the zoo. See Alicia have a pillow fight.'"

"But what'll keep all the other photogs from taking those shots?"

"They'll be able to get some, but they're not going to be allowed in stores where she shops, and they're definitely *not* getting in on the pillow fight."

"So these will be staged photos?"

Carla heard the disappointment in my voice. "Honey, if you want to be a celebrity photographer, you'll have to get used to staged photos."

I knew that, of course. Celebrities posed for Annie Leibovitz. I just needed to get over the surprise. "You said next week?"

"She's scheduled to come in Tuesday night. The *Late Show* tapes Wednesday afternoon. My guess is, you'll be shooting from Wednesday night until Friday night. She's flying back early Saturday morning."

"What about school?" I asked.

The phone line was silent. I wondered if Carla was considering how to answer that question. Or perhaps she was just trying to recover from the shock of being asked. Then she said, "My dear, you've just gone through a six-month dry spell. Now one of the hottest new stars on the planet has asked for *you*. She didn't ask for Annie. She didn't ask for Bruno or Howard. School, schmool. If this is what you want to do in life, make it happen."

She was so totally right. What was I thinking? This was the kind of gig I'd been dreaming about!

"I'm sorry," I stammered. "I don't know why I said that. I think I'm just so totally shocked that I don't know what to ask."

"How about, how much are they paying you?"

"They're *paying* me?" I blurted.

Carla chuckled. "Yes, Jamie, that's what people do

when they hire photographers. They pay them."

The phone call ended and I stood in Nasim's kitchen in a daze. It was a miracle! Just when I thought my career was on the autopsy table, someone had breathed life into the corpse! Had luck struck yet again, or was there some other explanation? I really didn't care. All I felt was relief. A weight had lifted. I was still in the ball game. This potential has-been had just been promoted to now-is.

That's when I noticed how quiet it had become. Nasim was no longer playing. I went back into the living room. He was sitting at the piano, staring at the sheet music. I had the feeling he was purposefully not looking at me. He said, "I was going to ask you what you thought."

In the silence that followed, his words reverberated around the room like a crescendo.

"I'm sorry," I began to say. "It was—"

"Business," Nasim ended the sentence for me with the same sarcastic bite my mother used to put on the word "career." For someone who hardly ever let his emotions show, it was obvious that he was fuming.

"Am I, like, being totally obnoxious?" I asked, hoping that he'd say no, that he understood how long it had been since I'd felt productive, and how important this was to me.

But he didn't say anything.

Nasim bid me a chilly farewell at his front door, standing just far enough away that I knew a good-bye kiss was out of the question. I left with a queasy, foreboding sensation in my stomach, hoping this wasn't some kind of momentous turning point in our relationship from which there was no going back. I didn't think he was being completely fair. Not only did he not understand how important this was to me, but I doubted he was aware of how the stress of the upcoming recital affected him. I decided to wait and talk to him about it after some time had passed and he'd had a chance to calm down.

My thoughts turned to the Alicia Howard gig. How amazing was this? Once again, my star was on the rise. I was going to meet and shoot Alicia Howard when she came to New York. Wait till Avy and the rest of the school found out!

"ARE YOU OKAY, MISS GORDON?" MARIA ASKS IN WILLOW'S kitchen after Rex departs. Realizing that I've been staring at the camera display with my mouth agape, I jerk my head up, at the same time flipping the camera, display down, on the counter. Maria scowls.

"Oh, yes," I stammer. "Fine, thanks." But a second later I pick up the camera with both hands, pressing it against my stomach, and hurry out of the kitchen. I feel like a duck at the pond who gets a big piece of bread and scurries off before the other ducks can take it away. But then I realize that if anyone sees me hurrying around holding my camera like this, they'll know in an instant that something is up.

To my left is a powder room, and I quickly slip inside and lock the door. I sit down and once again go through the shots that I didn't take. There are six altogether. Badly lit, awkwardly framed, and taken from odd angles—obviously candids taken by an amateur. But the subject matter more than makes up for the technical imperfections. These shots are what the media would call *explosive* and *ruinous*. If any of them ever gets out, Willow Twine's career is absolutely over. No questions asked. She couldn't possibly have known someone was taking them.

So now what? In my hands is the power to destroy one of the most famous celebrities on the planet. This is dynamite stuff. The ultimate money shot times ten. My *People* cover of Naomi Fine preggers would pale in comparison. I take a deep breath and try to convince myself that there is no rush. The pictures won't go anywhere without me. I have time to think. . . .

But all I do is stare down at the camera in my hands, questions racing through my head: *Are you making too much of this? Either erase or don't erase, right?*

Erasing is easy. Simple. Damage control completed. After all, Willow is now a friend. But if it's so easy, why won't my fingers move? I gaze down at the screen again and know why. In my hands, at my fingertips, is everything a paparazzo works for: the Ginormous Money Shot. Even though their quality is poor and I didn't take them, these photos are in my camera and that makes them mine.

My hands tremble slightly. With these shots, I would not only *make* news, I would *be* news.

Again.

I would be famous.

Again.

YOU WILL SIT ON THE BED WITH THE MACBOOK ON YOUR LAP,

gazing sadly at the last recorded images of your best friend. You've heard people say they hated their parents, but never with the vehemence with which Avy announces it.

You will dab the dampness from your cheeks and use the cuff of your shirt to blot the tears that have fallen onto the MacBook's keyboard. From the hall will come the sound of Alex's garbled voice, then a knock on your door. "Jamie?" your mother will say. "Can you come out here and help me with Alex?"

"In a minute, Mom." You just need to watch a little more.

On the screen, several moments will pass while Avy sits there, silent, brooding as if once again experiencing all that anger toward his parents. Then he will shake his head as if trying to get out of that rut, and ask, "Did you ever have any doubts about a career as an actor?"

He will brighten and pause, as if pleased at having been asked this question. After taking a sip from a glass of water on a table beside the chair, he'll answer, "Of course I did. But that almost didn't matter, because all I ever wanted was to be famous. I don't mind admitting it. No one just accidentally stumbles into stardom, and anyone who says they did is just a big fat Botoxed liar. You fight, you sweat, you claw your way up. No one gets to the top without having the flesh of a thousand other actors under their fingernails. Dog eat dog, baby. And as hard as it is getting up there, staying up there is even harder. Everybody wants to take you down. Everybody wants to be the next you. The pressure is enormous."

Having given this answer, he will purse his lips, furrow his forehead, and nod as if satisfied, then lean forward again and ask, "What do you think set you apart from the rest?"

You will feel a sad, wistful smile cross your lips. How poignantly ironic is this? On the MacBook screen, Avy will sit back and again prepare his answer. This time he will add gestures with his hands. "Honestly, it's hard to say. Everyone knows it takes hard work and persistence. You always feel like the odds are against you. Luck definitely plays a part. You just have to be in the right place at the right time."

Again, he will appear pleased with his answer and will lean forward to ask, "Does it ever get easier?"

He will answer, "Maybe when you go mega like Depp or Clooney. But for every Brad Pitt there are a ton of guys who had it in the palm of their hands and let it slip through their fingers. They had that one big hit. They made the cover of *People*. Maybe even an Oscar nomination for best supporting actor. But two flops later they were done. Gone. Not bankable. That's the scariest part."

You will pause the interview and wonder who Avy was practicing this for. Clearly someone had prepared questions ahead of time for him. But why ask Avy these questions? How would he know if it ever got any easier?

N,
So good to get a reply!!! You're right. You did tell me you'd be visiting friends of your parents' yesterday. Sorry I forgot. Too much going on! Glad you had a nice time with them.

So listen, what I'm going to tell you is top, Top, TOP secret. You can't tell anyone. I know you don't really care, which is why I can trust you ;-)

Yesterday Willow and I had breakfast (at 2 in the afternoon!). Just the two of us at a table beside the pool with fresh fruit and croissants! Willow's totally jazzed about getting the role in <u>The Pretenders</u>. Everyone says it's a phenomenal script. There's going to be a soundtrack CD, but it's not another bunch of her bubble-gum songs. She'll sing three serious love ballads. The rest are songs from other bands. The movie is supposed to start shooting next month. Because of Willow's visit to rehab, the film's producers forced her manager, Aaron Ives, to renegotiate her deal. Any hint of drugs or alcohol and she's gone. No ifs, ands, or buts. The producers can't afford to spend hundreds of millions of dollars on this movie and then have Willow destroy it with bad publicity.

N, she told me all of this herself! She really took me into her confidence! She said she hates going clubbing and not being able to have a drink, but all her friends have been totally supportive and won't drink in front of her. The movie company actually has spies! They'll know if she does anything she's not supposed to do. She said that in just about every restaurant and club she goes to there's someone being paid by the movie company to keep an eye on her. And plenty of actresses praying that she messes up so they can get her role.

And the one she's the most worried about? Alicia Howard. N, the things she said about Alicia, and how she got this far in her career, would make your face burn! Willow made me swear not to tell anyone. It would look really bad if people found out she was spreading rumors (even though she swears they're true!) about Alicia.

N, I know she has lots of friends she's known much longer than me, but I wonder if they understand the "business" side of her life the way I do. I think that's why she confided in me.

She said she was glad I was there because I seemed like a nice person who wouldn't stick a knife in her back. Not like so many other people who only want to be her friend because they think they can gain from it. She told me the pressure on her is huge. If The Pretenders is a success, she'll be back on top. If it's a flop, her career is toast. Then we talked about my photo assignment. She said it's really hard to be perfect for a whole week, and she hopes I'll understand. I guess she means that if I get a shot of her picking her nose or checking to make sure her pits don't smell, that I won't try to sell it on the side just to make a few extra bucks. I agreed, of course. It's not like selling a shot like that would further my career as a celebrity photographer, and it's not going to further her career as an actress, right? In the long term, neither of us would benefit.

After breakfast, Willow had all kinds of appointments, including costume fittings for The Pretenders and a script reading at the studio (I got to meet her co-star, Cody Patrick! He's gorgeous! Be very, very jealous, N!). So I took lots of shots for the exclusive.

Then guess where we had dinner? A cookout at Cody Patrick's beach house! Right on the Pacific Ocean! There were about fifty aspiring actresses and models there, and a bunch of Cody's guy friends.

(The female to male ratio was at least 3:1. The guys were loving it.)

But we didn't stay that long. Willow was tired. We came back, and she went to bed. In the guesthouse I stayed up and watched <u>Once</u>. Did you ever see it, N? OMG! It's the most romantic movie ever! We have to watch it together when I get back.

So here's the top secret. This morning I went into the kitchen, and the unfamiliar scent of cigarette smoke was in the air. Someone was sitting at the kitchen counter, a thin plume of smoke rising and spreading above him. He was bare-chested and had disheveled black hair, and on his back was a tattoo of a huge green dragon with a bright red tongue. On the other side of the kitchen, Maria wrinkled her nose disapprovingly. The smoke was pretty gross.

Can you guess who it was? Rex Dobro! In Willow's kitchen!!!! Bent over a coffee and cigarette. I froze until he turned, smiled soulfully at me, and said, "Hey." N, I've never heard anyone stretch out a one-syllable word the way he can.

The word poured out of his throat so slowly, most people could have completed an entire sentence in the same time. He rubbed a puffy eye. "You're the kid photographer?"

Ouch! I felt a little like I'd just been dissed. I mean, maybe I am a kid photographer, but did he have to say it? Anyway, I came back with, "So I've been told."

"Where's your camera?" he asked.

"It was amputated last night. You know those surgeons. They just love to cut." (N, wasn't I, like, just sooooo clever? Kid photographer, my foot!)

"Hmm." Rex took a drag and snorted on the exhale. "Funny," he said without a smile.

Maria brought me a cup of coffee. She shot her eyes at Rex, then gave me a quick sour look. I had a feeling it was more than just the cigarette smoke that she disapproved of.

So guess who trudged in next? Willow! Wrapped in a black silk robe, her hair as disheveled as Rex's. She draped her arm over his shoulder and pressed her face into his for a long kiss. Morning breath, cigarettes, and coffee didn't seem to bother her one bit.

She slid onto the stool between Rex and me. "No photos?"

"No camera." I raised my hands to show that they were empty.

"You're the best." Willow put her arm around my shoulder and gave me a hug, then turned back to Rex and gently nudged him with her elbow. "How you doin'?"

"Not bad, you?" Rex drawled.

"Happy, I think."

Rex raised an eyebrow. "You <u>think</u>?"

"No, I know," Willow corrected herself, and kissed him on the cheek.

It was definitely time to leave the love puppies alone, so I left. But N, you realize how amazing this is? Rexlow is back together! It's HUGE!

But don't forget. This is TOP SECRET! XOXOXO!!! Hit me back!

I'M SITTING IN THE PINK POWDER ROOM IN WILLOW'S MANSION—

a digital gold mine in my hands—hearing voices in my head.

Me: "Can I really do this? Destroy Willow's career in order to advance mine?"

Carla: "Darling, are you crazy? This is your ticket. Everything you've dreamed of since day one. People would kill for this kind of opportunity. You think if it was the other way around—if Willow Twine needed to wreck your career to advance her own—she'd hesitate for a second?"

"But Willow and I are friends."

"Oh, please! You've known her for exactly one week."

"You don't know. You haven't been out here with us."

"My dear, they were calling me an old-timer in this business back when you were still in Pampers. I've seen and heard it all. Believe me, I know."

My BlackBerry vibrates. I slide it out of my pocket and check the number. Speak of the devil. It's Carla. I almost answer, but something stops me. We spoke yesterday. She said we'd speak again when I got back to New York. So why is she suddenly calling?

Instead of answering, I let the phone take a message and then listen to it. "Jamie, sweetheart. Wuzzup, girl? So listen, there's a rumor going around that Willow was partying with old Rexxy last night. Any truth to that? You wouldn't happen to have any shots, would you? Let me know, because those shots could be worth their weight in gold."

Huh? I stare at the BlackBerry, seriously puzzled. This is totally beyond strange. How in the world could Carla know that Willow and Rex were partying last night? That was supposed to be top top secret.

The BlackBerry rings again. This time it's Edie McGovern, one of the editors from the *Weekly Dish* website. Again I don't answer and wait instead to listen to the message. "Hey, Jamie, s'up, babe? Heard you're out in LA hanging with Willow. Any truth to the rumor she was out with Rex last night? We'd give any pix you've got big money and big play. Here's my direct line in case you don't have it."

Even as I listen to this message, another call is coming in, and I listen to that message next. It's from Suzie Feld at the gossip website *Hear It Here First.* "Jamie, darling, listen, there's word on the street that you may have hit the mother lode. Whatever you do, talk to me before you sell those shots to anyone else. I could make this huge for you. Call me as soon as you get this message. I'm giving you my personal cell phone number, the one I never give out."

I've hardly finished listening to that message when the phone vibrates again. It's Carla. "Jamie, what's going on out there? I'm swamped with calls about these photos you're supposed to have. They're going nuts. I'm getting offers sight unseen. You have to call me immediately."

The phone keeps vibrating, but I stop paying attention. How do all these people on the other side of the country know about Rex and Willow? Why do they think I have photos when I only found out about all this a few minutes ago? It's as if they knew about it *before* I did. How is that possible?

Rapid footsteps are approaching in the hall outside the powder room. I hear Willow's personal assistant, Doris Remlee, urgently asking, "Zach, have you seen Jamie Gordon this morning?"

"Yeah, uh—" Zach begins.

"Where?" Doris impatiently cuts him short.

"Out by the pool."

"When?"

"A little while ago. She went into the kitchen. I guess she was getting coffee or something. Oh, and she asked me if I'd seen her camera."

"Oh, God! Did you?"

"Well, yeah, I told her I thought I saw it on the kitchen counter. Why? What's going on?"

"Go out to the front gate and make sure it stays closed. No one is to come in or go out, understand? No one. Then get over to the guesthouse. See if she's there. If she is, grab her and don't let go. Under any circumstances. You hold on to her *and* her camera. If she's not there, search her things. I want every camera she has."

"Why? What's going on?" Zach asks.

"Just do it!" Doris shouts.

Footsteps slap as Zach leaves. This is crazy. Obviously Doris knows about the photos. But how? How can she know about them when I just found them on my camera? Now other footsteps approach at a run and a voice high and tight with panic asks, "Does anyone know where she is?"

It's Willow. And she's hysterical.

"No, but she can't have gone far," Doris answers. "Zach says she was here just a moment ago."

"We have to find her," Willow gasps. "Oh, my God,

we *have* to! Have you checked the guesthouse?"

"Zach's doing that right now," Doris says. When another set of footsteps approaches she commands, "Daphne, I want you to disable the Internet connection immediately. Wireless and hardwire."

"That'll disconnect the television and phone," Daphne counters.

"I don't care if it disconnects the plumbing, just do it!" snaps Doris. "And make sure that includes the guesthouse."

"Wait, Daphne." It's Willow's voice. "Is it possible to transfer photos from a camera to a BlackBerry and transmit them?"

"If you had the right software. But it's not a common thing to do. So it sounds like we think Jamie has some pictures we don't want to get out?"

"That's exactly what it sounds like," says Doris. "Go disable the Internet. And if you see Jamie, grab her and call me immediately."

From the other side of the powder room door I hear footsteps depart and assume that's Daphne leaving. Which means Doris and Willow are still out in the hall.

"Don't worry," Doris says as soothingly as possible. "Stay calm. She's not going anywhere."

"When I find that little bitch," Willow growls under her breath, "I will shove that camera down her pudgy little throat."

Her words make me wince. *So much for being friends.*

"Where's Sam?" she asks.

"Haven't seen him this morning," Doris answers.

"For God's sake!" Willow blurts.

Faint electronic beeps follow. "Sam? It's Doris. Get over here immediately. We need you now. I'll explain when you get here. And if by any chance you spot Jamie Gordon on the way, grab her and don't let go."

Another beep.

"I'm going out to look for her," Doris announces. "Will you be okay?"

"I'll be better when this is over," Willow answers in a quavering voice.

A moment passes. Then Doris says, "I'll take care of this, darling. In the meantime, there's someone else you need to deal with."

Footsteps leave. But only one set. I assume they're Doris's, which means Willow's still out there in the hall. Why? What's she doing? Is she staring at the powder room door right now? Is she about to reach for the knob and open it?

SUMMER IN THE CITY. SO HOT AND HUMID I SOMETIMES TOOK TWO or three showers a day to get the sticky grime off my skin. Nasim had gone to Iran to visit cousins, and Avy spent July living in a college dorm in LA attending some superfancy summer performing arts program. I think it was his parents' way of trying to make up for not letting him take the role on *Rich and Poor*.

I was so happy to hear his voice when he called and said he wanted to meet for dinner at El Caribe, our favorite cheapo Cuban-Chinese hole-in-the-wall. We ordered shredded beef, some fried plantains, and a heaping plate of black beans and yellow rice. Avy was tanned and glowing with good health. His curly brown hair had been lightened by the California sun. Something else looked different as well.

"Is it my imagination, or have you gotten taller and thinner?" I asked.

He grinned with delight. Was it also my imagination that his teeth looked whiter?

"Grew one and one-quarter inches this year," he said. "Doctor says I might actually reach five ten before I'm done."

"How was the program? How long have you been back from LA?"

"It was great. Got back a week ago."

I felt a frown emerge. "A week? Why didn't you call sooner?"

"I'll tell you in a minute. First, how's the job?"

"Okay," I answered with an unenthusiastic shrug. I was interning for the summer at a photography studio, mostly airbrushing pimples off newlyweds' faces, making double chins disappear, and thinning plump arms.

"Gone on any stakeouts?" Avy asked.

"Not many. The rich and famous are away for the summer. It's been really hot, grimy, and slow. I haven't sold a shot in months."

"What about that Alicia Howard exclusive?"

"Nothing came of it," I answered with disappointment. The memory of that experience still stung. I'd been so excited, and I'd had to argue so hard to get Mom to let me take the days off from school. I think she only relented because I wore her down until she was too tired to say no. But in the end it turned out to be a great big nothing. I took the two and a half days off from school and shot a zillion pictures. Alicia was always nice to me, but also sort of distant, and it quickly became obvious that even though I was fifteen too and she'd specifically asked for me to do the shoot, she was going to treat me the way she would any other photographer.

"They paid you, didn't they?" Avy asked.

"Yes, but you know what?" I said. "That's almost beside the point. I really wanted them to use those pictures."

"Did they ever tell you why they didn't?"

I shook my head. "Carla said it was Alicia's money and she could do whatever she wanted with those shots. Maybe her plans changed, or maybe she just felt ugly that week." I knew I sounded glum, so I added, "Hey, it's all part of the business, you know? It'll get better in the fall when everyone comes back."

Avy nodded and leaned his elbows on the worn gray Formica table. His eyes were shining. It was obvious that he was excited about something. "I'm going back to LA."

"For August?" I asked.

"For . . . *ever*."

"You got a role?" I asked excitedly. "On a series or something?"

"Not yet."

The excitement drained away. "Then . . . why?"

"Because LA's where it's happening, Jamie. It's where I've got to be."

"But you live here. What about school?"

He took out some tickets for trains from New York to LA. I gave him a puzzled look.

"It's real, Wonder Girl," he said. "The reason you haven't heard from me is, I've been busy all week selling stuff on eBay and finding an apartment on Craigslist."

I stared at him uncertainly. "Avy, you're fifteen."

"No one has to know that. Look, it's a done deal. I'm going."

You could have scraped me off the greasy linoleum floor. I was stunned. "Why?"

He talked about how certain he was that he could make it in Hollywood. Acting was all he'd ever wanted to do and was all he would ever want to do. He talked about how scared and excited he was, and how deep down he really, truly believed he could make it on his own. He talked and talked, as if he needed to convince himself as much as he did me.

The shredded beef, yellow rice, and black beans sat half-finished on the table between us. Finally there didn't seem to be anything more to say, which was strange when it came to Avy and me. Usually we could talk forever. We paid the bill and stepped out into the noisy, humid New

York night. Cabs and buses trundled past and we stood on the sidewalk hugging tearfully and promising each other we'd text a hundred times a day.

"The next time I come back here," he said, "it'll be either first class or private jet. And I'll tell them the only photographer I want taking my picture is you. And that's the way it's going to be, Wonder Girl. You and me. We're going all the way to the top together."

He gave me one last hug, then squeezed my arms and stared intently into my eyes. "You'll see. It's gonna be great." He turned and strode away down the sidewalk like someone determined to go somewhere. Like someone who knew where he was going.

But to tell you the truth, I thought he'd be back in time to start tenth grade at Herrin with the rest of us.

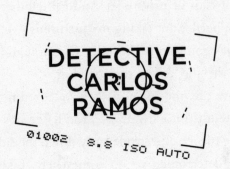

DETECTIVE CARLOS RAMOS

01002 8.8 ISO AUTO

I never even thought about celebrity stalkers until that Chapman kid shot John Lennon. What a terrible, senseless tragedy. I mean, I might not have agreed with Lennon's politics, but there's no denying the enormous contribution he made to music.

But the one that really got me was when that actress Rebecca Schaeffer from that show *My Sister Sam* was murdered. I used to watch it with my kids. Here's this cute young woman, twenty-two years old, who everyone agreed was on her way to really big things, and this nut gets her address from the Department of Motor Vehicles, then goes over to her house and shoots her.

My kids were devastated. They'd say, "Daddy, why did that man do that to her?" And what could I say? How do you explain to kids that there are some things in life that make no sense?

And then there was that tennis player, Monica Seles, one of the top players in the world, and during a tennis match this obsessed fan jumps on the courts and stabs her in the back with a nine-inch knife. Again, just the utter senselessness of it.

And the thing is, these attackers know they're going to be caught. Most of the time they don't even resist. They want the world to know they did it. As if it's the only way people will ever know they existed.

Some people say that if you want to become famous, that's a risk you have to face, but I disagree. People shouldn't have to fear for their lives on a daily basis just because they've accomplished something extraordinary. And that's especially true here in Los Angeles, where there are so many stars. The LAPD created the Threat Management Unit because we all know how important it is that stars feel safe. This town depends on the movie business, and if the stars can't feel comfortable here, we're in trouble.

But for me personally, it goes beyond that. These stars get so much publicity. So many people—especially young people—follow their lives. These days life is difficult and frightening enough for kids. They don't need to be exposed to random acts of murderous insanity.

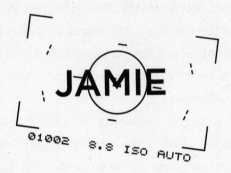

ON THE MACBOOK SCREEN, AVY WILL GROW PENSIVE AGAIN, PLACING his elbow on his thigh then making a fist and pressing his lips against it. You can almost feel the mood darkening inside him as he returns to the subject of his parents and says, "But you've said in other interviews that they actually tried to stop you from becoming an actor."

Puzzled, you will pause the video. *Other interviews?* You're not aware of Avy having done any other interviews. Is it possible that he did and didn't tell you? But who would have interviewed him? And why?

Once again you will start the video. "They did," Avy will reply to his own question. "They tried to stop me.

Maybe that's why I worked so hard to succeed. Maybe that's why I made it. I just had to prove them wrong."

On the screen, Avy will smirk and shake his head, rise from the chair, and come toward the camera. The video will become blurry and wobbly and then go black. This is where the interview will end. You will stare at the MacBook screen, replaying Avy's last words in your head. *"Maybe that's why I worked so hard to succeed. Maybe that's why I made it. I just had to prove them wrong."*

It will make no sense. Avy wasn't a success. He never "made it." Except for the few commercials he did here in New York before he went to LA, he never even came close.

And then it will hit you. *Avy made this up. The whole thing. This wasn't an interview he was preparing to give. This is the interview . . . he only dreamed of giving.*

Your insides will wrench, and new tears will blur your vision. Feeling wretched, you will close the computer and let it rest on your lap. Poor Avy. Your parents—at least, your mother—may have given you a hard time about what you wanted to do too. But at least you had the feeling that they cared.

Tears will fall against the MacBook's white plastic cover as a rush of regret and self-recrimination floods over you. In the end, Avy had no one. He was all alone, giving interviews to himself because no one else cared. And where were you, Jamie Gordon? You could have made a much bigger effort to stay in touch with him after he ran off to LA. Avy was your closest friend. Lots of girls had female best friends, but for you it was Avy as far back as you can remember. He was always such a good friend to you. Were you such a good friend to him?

No.

You were so busy thinking about yourself, yourself, yourself, and your career.

N,

Just that one short e-mail is all I get? I wish you'd write again. It's spring vacation. Are you really that busy?

Anyway, out here it just gets crazier and crazier. I was waiting in the guesthouse to find out what the plans for the day were when guess who knocked on the French doors? Willow!

She asked, did I have a moment?

"No, Willow, I'm really busy. Can you come back later?" (JOKE!)

We sat on the porch, and she smiled impishly and said, "Pretty wild about Rex coming back, huh? I really don't know what to do about him. He said all that stuff about him and Dominika Bartoli is just hype. I want to believe him, but I just don't know."

I couldn't believe she, the super star, was confiding in me. It was definitely one of those "this can't be real" moments, and I considered pinching myself to see if I was dreaming. I mean, Willow Twine was asking me for relationship advice?

So, N, what could I say? I told her to take it slow. I mean, is that the ultimate piece of generic relationship advice or what? But Willow looked at me like I was Moses on the mountain.

"You're so right!" she said. "Like, what's the rush?"

Know what I think? Maybe someone like Willow is so used to getting everything she wants exactly when she wants it that she just isn't used to the idea of waiting for anything.

But there you have it, N. I had a ♥2♥ with Willow Twine!

I only wish I could have a ♥2♥ with you! XOXOXOXOXO

SEPTEMBER ARRIVED AND AVY DIDN'T. HE'D KEPT HIS WORD ABOUT going back to LA and staying there. It was hard to imagine being at Herrin without him. We'd been together since kindergarten, and the thought of school without my best friend and confidant was a lonely prospect. The night before classes started, I called him.

"Hey, s'up, Wonder Girl?" he answered.

"Know what tomorrow is?" I asked.

"Uh . . . first day of the rest of our lives?"

"First day of school."

The line went silent for a moment. Then Avy said

almost gleefully, "I *told* you I wasn't coming back. You didn't believe me, right?"

It was true. Although now it struck me that the prospect of school without Avy was so uninviting that maybe I hadn't *wanted* to believe him. "What do your parents say?"

"You'll love this. Know how they've been totally crazed about me being out here? Like, even threatening to hire a private detective to bring me home? Well, all of a sudden they've decided to become supportive. They want me to enroll in the Professional Children's Academy and find a better place to live. Can you believe it?"

"That's . . . great! I guess," I said, trying to hide my disappointment that he really, truly wasn't coming back.

"We'll see," Avy said with cautious optimism. "Could be the old reverse psychology trick. Like, they think if they go along with what I want I'll be more likely to get it out of my system and come home."

"I don't know, Avy. Enrolling you in the Professional Children's Academy doesn't sound like reverse psychology. It sounds like maybe you've convinced them that you're serious."

"Yeah, right." He suddenly sounded bitter. "Too bad they didn't feel that way when I was offered that role on *Rich and Poor*."

"Anything new on the acting front?" I asked.

"I've got some things cooking, but August was slow.

Everyone says it always picks up in the fall. So, what about you? Sell any shots lately?"

"The scene still hasn't kicked into gear here, either," I said. "But it will. I'm not worried."

"How's Nasim? How was his trip to Iran?"

This was another irksome and distressing part of my life. I told him that Nasim had come home from Iran the week before and hadn't called. I'd waited two days and then called him. "He acted like nothing was wrong, but I could tell something was. Remember I told you about what happened last spring? When he was practicing for his recital and I got that call from Carla? It's like he's never really forgiven me for that."

"And you've talked to him about it, right?"

"A bunch of times. He keeps saying it's all right and he's gotten past it, but he doesn't *act* like it's all right."

Avy was silent. Then he said, "I wish I knew what to say, Jamie. It sucks when you know someone you really care about is holding back. 'Cause there's no way you can make them talk. So every time you see him you feel like it's hovering there between you. The proverbial albatross around your neck."

Tears threatened to well up in my eyes. Avy was so great. How many people do you know who really listen and think about you like that? He was special, and that only made me miss him more. "Your parents aren't the only ones who want you to come back, Avy. I miss you too."

"Yeah, I miss you," he said, his tone changing. "You know, seriously, Wonder Girl, it's not all fun and games out here. It gets lonely a lot. And there are so many people who can't be bothered with you. You never feel more like a nobody than when you're trying to be somebody and everyone's closing doors in your face. Tell you the truth, I really am glad my parents want me to go to the Professional Children's Academy. At least I'll be with people like myself."

"Or you could just come back," I said hopefully.

"There's no point. This is where I have to be. I mean, I know it's gonna be hard, but I have to do it. And I will do it. Know how I know? Because I'm willing to do whatever it takes. I mean . . ." He paused, and I got the feeling he was debating whether to tell me something. "Guess where I'm going next week. Tijuana."

"Why?"

"To have some work done."

"What kind of work?" I asked, not understanding.

"Nose and chin."

I nearly dropped my cell phone. "Oh, Avy, you're not serious!"

He was quiet for a moment, as if that wasn't the reaction he'd hoped for. Then he said, "You don't understand, Jamie. It's different out here."

"Your nose and chin are fine," I said.

"It's not a big deal. Really."

"It's mutilation, Avy."

"If that's true, then just about everyone out here is mutilated," he said.

I was glad he couldn't see the brief smile that came and went from my lips. But just because he could make a joke about it didn't make it any less serious. I wanted him to know how extremely opposed I was to someone our age having cosmetic work done. We talked for a while longer, but nothing I said could make him change his mind. Avy clung to the idea like it was a life preserver . . . or a magic bullet that would alter the trajectory of his career.

From there the conversation moved on to the safe and comfortable zone of celebrity gossip, a place where Avy and I could have easily dwelled for hours were it not for the limitations of our cell phone batteries. But deep inside I couldn't help thinking that something was seriously wrong.

I WAS HYPER. CARLA HAD CALLED AND SAID SHE HAD SOMETHING HUGE, and now I was sitting in the waiting area of her office, hands pressed between my knees, feet tapping nervously. My career had been stalled for nearly a year. She'd said on the phone that this wouldn't be like the Alicia Howard thing. It would be better. Whatever "it" was, I needed it badly.

Carla skipped out of her office practically hyperventilating, plunked herself down on the couch, took my hands in hers and patted them. "You, my darling, are about to have your dreams come true."

My heart beat harder. I already knew that Willow

Twine's manager, Aaron Ives, and her publicist, Heather Taylor, were in Carla's office, waiting to speak to me. What I didn't know was why. A month earlier a fresh-faced Willow had emerged happy and smiling from rehab with a planned concert tour, dozens of interviews and TV appearances. Rex Dobro had been photographed with a strictly B-role actress named Dominika Bartoli. When asked about him, Willow said they were out of touch. It was as if he'd never happened.

"Just be your normal sweet adorable self," Carla counseled on the couch outside her office. "That's what they like about you."

"*They?*" I repeated.

"You'll see." Pulling me by the hand, Carla led me into the office.

Inside, Aaron Ives sat at the desk, talking to someone on Carla's MacPro. I recognized him from photographs. This was the man who'd made Willow who she was. Actually, they'd made each other. Aaron was just starting out in the talent agency business when he discovered Willow, so everything he'd become he owed to her. And vice versa.

"Give me a second, sweetheart, she's here," he said in a British accent. He looked up from the computer, smiled at me—revealing unnaturally straight white teeth—and extended his hand. "Jamie? I'm Aaron Ives. Delighted to meet you."

"Thanks, me, too," I said, shaking his hand. "I mean, I'm delighted to meet *you,* since I've already met me."

He smiled as if anything I'd said would have been utterly adorable. "Have a seat." He gestured to the couch, where, for the first time, I noticed Heather Taylor, a small, redheaded woman wearing a black pantsuit.

"Hi," I said.

Willow's publicist gave me the old "we're so very glad to meet you" routine. I sat down beside her on the couch. Carla took a chair near the door. I thought it was strange that this was her office and yet Aaron Ives was sitting at her desk, using her Mac, and acting as if it were his office. But maybe that was how things worked in showbiz.

"So, Jamie." Aaron leaned his elbows on the desk and intertwined his fingers as if in prayer. "Congratulations."

"Uh, thanks, but for what exactly?" I asked.

Aaron turned to Carla, who smiled as if once again I'd just said something utterly adorable.

"For accomplishing so much at such a young age," he said. "It's not everyone who gets profiled in *New York Weekly* and has a *People* magazine cover at the age of fifteen."

"Thank you." I couldn't imagine where this was leading and had to stop myself from blurting out that I wished he'd cut to the chase and just tell me. With that blindingly white, unnaturally even smile, Aaron leaned and placed his elbows on his thighs. "How would you like to do an exclusive on Willow?"

"But not like what Carla told us happened with Alicia Howard," Heather quickly interjected. "We're looking at a magazine spread. We're talking to *People, US Weekly,* and *Seventeen.* They're all interested."

To avoid betraying the way I felt, which was totally stunned, I tried to act cool and asked the first thing that popped into my head: "Willow's coming to New York?"

"Oh, no," said Heather. "You'll be going out there. She wants you to stay with her."

"In Los Angeles?" I asked uncertainly.

"That's right," said Aaron. "In her mansion."

Stay with Willow Twine—the biggest teen star in the world—in her mansion? I glanced at Carla, and she nodded eagerly as if to assure me that it wasn't a joke. That's when my total astonishment got the better of me and I asked the kind of question you're not supposed to ask: "Why me?"

"Brilliant question," Aaron said in a way that let me know he'd been waiting for me to ask. "Willow's known about you ever since that *New York Weekly* story. You may recall she was also in that issue."

I nodded.

"And you know, of course, that's she's been through rather a rough patch recently. The unfortunate accident and the run-in with the authorities, and then rehab. But she's put all that behind her now. She's ready to make her comeback, and she's got the perfect vehicle. A terrific new movie, *The Pretenders*. I can't tell you much more than that right now, but believe me, in a few weeks it will be huge entertainment news. For now we just want young women, I mean, girls, to know that Willow is still one of them. What better way to do that than to have someone close to their own age spend time with her, get to know her, literally become her friend, and document a week in the life of Willow Twine."

Aaron paused to let the words sink in. *A Week in the Life of Willow Twine . . . by Jamie Gordon.* Carla, Aaron, and Heather looked at me expectantly. For a moment I was so dazzled—by the suggestion, by his accent, by the blinding brightness of his teeth—that I didn't realize they were waiting for my answer.

"Jamie?" Carla finally said.

I forced myself out of the fog. "Uh, yeah, I mean, thank you *so* much. I'm thrilled. I mean, yes! Great, let's do it!" I said. Was there any other way to reply?

"Brilliant!" Aaron turned the MacPro to face me. On the screen was a desk and an empty chair. Behind the chair was a bookcase lined with plaques, statuettes, and photos. "Willow, darling?" he said.

For a few seconds nothing happened. Then a woman sat down in the chair. She was wearing a thick white terrycloth robe and pulling a large light blue comb through her straight, wet hair. She looked very familiar, but without makeup it took an extra second for me to recognize her. "Hi, there," she said with a smile.

"Uh, hi." I concentrated on not sounding utterly awestruck and bedazzled.

"Nice to meet you," she said.

"You, too," I said. "I mean, thank you so much for thinking of me."

"So, you like our idea?" Willow asked.

"It sounds great," I said.

"I think it's going to be so much fun," Willow gushed as if she were as excited as me. "We'll spend the whole week together. Just you and me. We'll really get to know each other. It'll be such a blast."

We grinned at each other on the computer. Then Willow reached toward the screen. "Gotta go, okay? See you soon."

The screen went gray. Aaron Ives swiveled it away.

"Uh, okay," Heather the publicist said, more to Carla than to me. "Just so we're straight up front, there are a couple of conditions. Obviously, it can't just be Jamie and Willow all week. Willow's got all kinds of appointments and meetings. But we are proposing that Jamie stay on the property and spend as much time as possible with her. As far as the pictures go, we'd like to get past the typical photo op and really let Jamie have the opportunity for some intimate candids, but obviously we also need to have some control."

"I'm sure she understands," Aaron said in a terse way that made it clear that these details could be discussed at another time. "So, you're on board, Jamie?"

"Definitely," I said.

"Brilliant." Willow's manager nodded at Carla, who rose from her chair and said to me, "Come on, Jamie, I'll walk you out."

Aaron and Heather stood, and once again we shook hands. Out in the waiting room, I gave Carla a quizzical look and whispered, "Why would Willow want to hang out with me? Isn't she, like, three or four years older?"

"Try four or five years." Carla dropped her voice to imply confidentiality. "But my guess is, that's got a lot to do with it."

"You mean, youth by association?" I asked.

"Right. It gives the whole project a younger feel. At least, that's the way Heather wants to spin it. It's all about reassuring Willow's fan base that even though she and Rex Dobro were hot and heavy, she's still the same sweet, virginal girl singer and actress that they've come to love and admire. There's just one thing you have to do. Get your mom to let you go out to Hollywood for a week."

E-MAIL TO
NASIM

01002 8.8 ISO AUTO

N,
Did you get my voice mail? I hope
the silent treatment isn't your way
of punishing me. It doesn't seem like
something you'd do. It's really hard
to be so far away and not know what
you're thinking. Especially after what
happened. Please call back or write.
   Anyway, it's gone from crazy
to bizarre here. Everything has
changed. Willow's canceled all her
appointments. Her personal assistant,

Doris, is stalking around with a huge frown on her face. A whole new group of people, mostly guys, have shown up, and the scene around here has gone from "Girls just want to have fun" to "Guys just want to jump girls." The stink of cigarette smoke is in the air, and abandoned glasses and beer bottles are everywhere.

There's a morose silence, almost a sense of doom, among the staff. This morning Willow's publicist, Heather Taylor, came to the front gate but wasn't allowed in. Sam's here, but no matter how vigilant he tries to be, people seem to disappear into the pool house or some bathroom and come back giggling, smirking, or just plain hyper.

I was in the kitchen having a salad with Doris before when Willow and Rex came in and announced that they wanted to have a party. Willow dictated a list of things she wanted Doris to order--party platters, beverages, etc.

"Better toss in some beer," Rex

added. "Maybe a case of Red Stripe and a case of Dos Equis. Half a dozen bottles of Patrón Silver and Ketel One."

When Doris hesitated, Willow snapped, "Do what he says."

When she's with Rex, there's something about Willow's voice and body language that's different. Is it adoration? The need to please? At the same time, she's become bratty and demanding to everyone else.

It's very weird, N. Maybe you'll write back and tell me what you think? Isn't that what you said you'd do?

ONLY THE SLEAZE, PLEASE!
LA SHOCKER! TEEN SENSATION
WILLOW TWINE ENTERS REHAB!

Less than forty-eight hours after crashing her Mercedes into the side of a garbage truck, teen superstar Willow Twine has voluntarily entered an exclusive LA rehab facility for what a spokesperson said was an "accidental" dependence to prescription painkillers.

This is the latest surprise in a series of bizarre developments that began early Sunday morning when Twine, accompanied by rocker boyfriend Rex Dobro—both apparently under the influence of drugs—sideswiped three cars and ran a red light before crashing into the side of the truck.

Police responding to the scene reported finding marijuana, pills, and a bag containing an unidentified white powder. The young actress was taken into custody and charged with possession of illegal substances and driving while impaired. Within hours, mug shots of Twine with stringy hair, a swollen split lip, and black eye from the crash were circulating on the Internet.

At the arraignment later that morning, Twine's manager, Aaron Ives, posted bail and handed out a typewritten statement allegedly from Dobro stating that he was responsible for the drugs. Surrounded by a phalanx of friends and supporters, Twine was whisked from the courtroom into a waiting car.

Many assumed that Ives would keep his star under wraps until the situation died down and was forgotten, but the next afternoon Rexlow was surrounded by an army of paparazzi after they were spotted shopping on Rodeo Drive. Dobro further aggravated the situation by getting into a fight with one of the photogs, and then Willow made a garbled and rambling statement about the evils of the paparazzi. Within the hour the clip was all over TV and the Internet and was followed by an even more incomprehensible and befuddled statement on Willow's website that was apparently intended to explain what she'd meant but instead left her fans scratching their heads and her enemies making snide comparisons to Britney and Lindsay.

A few hours later her publicist issued the announcement that Willow was going into rehab after "accidentally" becoming addicted to the prescription painkillers she'd been taking for a mysterious back injury that had never been mentioned before.

WHEN I SAW THE NEWS ON MY BLACKBERRY, I ACTUALLY CUT CLASS to call Avy from the washroom. Weeks had passed since we'd last connected. I'd spoken to him after he returned from Tijuana, but when I asked him to send me some shots of his new look, he said he wanted to wait until the swelling went down. The phone rang for a long time, and just when I expected to get his outgoing message, he answered with a yawn. "Hello?"

"Did you hear about Willow?" I gasped.

"Huh? Jamie? What time is it?" He sounded groggy.

"Two o'clock here, so it must be eleven there."

"Oh, man. I—" He coughed for a few seconds, then

cleared his throat. "I feel like I just went to bed."

"Well, wake up and smell the gossip! Willow's going into rehab!"

"Hmm." Avy sounded less than interested. I was shocked. This was the kind of thing we'd once spent hours dishing about. I wanted him to be interested. I needed him to still care about the things we used to care about. "Uh, know what, Jamie? Let me get some coffee and call you right back, okay?"

School ended, and Avy still hadn't called back. I went to a stakeout outside the federal court building downtown and stood on the cold marble steps for three hours with a dozen other photogs waiting for Blake Bloxon to come out, only to learn from a limo driver that the court appearance of the world's richest deadbeat dad had been postponed to another day.

Avy called around 8:00 p.m., six hours after he said he'd get coffee and call me right back. But at least he sounded more like himself. "Hey, Wonder Girl! Willow's in rehab! Can you believe it?"

"Oh, it's classic!" I gasped, delighted that I had the old Avy back. "Just what everyone predicted would happen if she took up with Rex!"

"From superstar to fallen woman," Avy said, and coughed.

"Well, not quite. More like a bump in the road, don't you think?"

"I don't know, Jamie. Have you checked out Facebook and some of the gossip sites? There's suddenly a lot of anti-Willow stuff out there. Think about it. If you're the mother of an eleven-year-old tweenybopper, do you want your daughter cheering for a rehabber with a rap sheet?"

"Even if Rex takes the blame for the drugs?" I asked.

"He wasn't driving. She was."

"You really think fans are that fickle?"

Avy's answer came after a spasm of deep, gurgling coughs. "Whoa, Wonder Girl, what alternative universe are *you* living in? Of course they're that fickle. Especially when they know Alicia Howard's waiting in the wings."

"Are you sick?" I asked while I Googled Alicia Howard on my MacBook.

"Nah, just a little phlegmy."

I found Alicia's website. "Listen to this. She's issued a special statement: 'I can only express my greatest admiration and concern for Willow. She was my number one idol as a girl. I wish her the best and hope she has a speedy recovery.'"

"Alicia's probably salivating so hard her handlers are looking for mops," Avy quipped.

I had to laugh. "Good one, Avy. Personally, I like the line, 'She was my number one idol as a girl.' Such a sweet backhanded dig at Willow's age."

"Come on, who's kidding who?" Avy asked. "If the

two of them were standing at the edge of a cliff and Willow began to lose her balance, Alicia would be more than happy to reach out . . . and give her a push."

"Except it looks like Rex has done it for her," I said.

Avy coughed, then cleared his throat. "True, that."

The velocity of gossip started to wane. "So, what's up?" I asked. "What have you been doing?"

"Same old, same old. I'm doing the academy thing, and Janice takes Sean and Brian and me to auditions—"

"Wait. Who are Janice, Sean, and Brian?"

"Sean and Brian are my roommates. Janice is Brian's mom. She's like our house mother and chaperone."

"So you moved?" I asked.

"Oh, yeah, didn't I tell you? My parents arranged for me to live in Starwood. It's where all the showbiz kids live. We're all at the Professional Children's Academy."

"But wait, if you're at the academy, how come you were sleeping when I called this morning?"

"Oh, yeah. Uh, um, I stayed home today because I've been kind of run-down. Between school and auditions and everything." He coughed again. It sounded deep and guttural.

"Seriously, Avy, are you okay?" I asked.

"Yeah, yeah. I've just had this bug for a couple of days. It'll go away. So, what's going on with you, Wonder Girl? How's New York's youngest paparazzo? Oops, I meant celebrity photographer."

I told him it had been really slow, and that things with Nasim seemed okay but I could never really tell what he was thinking. Once again, the conversation seemed to wane in a way it never had before. Avy coughed and cleared his throat. "So, uh, that's really crazy about Willow. Thanks for the update. Uh, I gotta go, Jamie. Let's talk again soon, okay?"

"Okay," I said. The line went dead. Maybe it was my imagination, but for the first time ever I felt like there was something more than just physical distance separating me from my best friend.

01002 8.8 ISO AUTO

"NO," MOM SAID. SHE, DAD, AND I WERE SITTING AT THE KITCHEN table. Alex was in the den watching TV.

"But this would be a huge step in my career," I said.

Mom's face tightened as if she still hated that word but had finally come to accept that she could do nothing about it. I turned to Dad and gave him a pleading look. Knowing I'd need his support, I'd asked him to stop by.

"I don't think you're being fair, Carol," he said.

"It's going to be over spring vacation, so I won't miss any school," I added. "You know you hate the idea of me being a paparazzo. Here's a chance for me to really establish myself as a celebrity photographer."

Mom looked at Dad. "She's not even sixteen years old. You can't be serious about letting her go all the way to the other side of the country to spend a week with a clearly unstable person who has a well-documented drug and alcohol problem."

"Willow's cleaned herself up," I said.

That drew another long, dramatic, "give me break" sigh from my mother.

"Seriously, Mom, she had to," I said. "Her whole career is in danger of going down the tubes. This assignment is part of the effort to save it."

"Am I allowed to ask why, out of all the photographers in the world, she chose you?" Mom asked.

I explained the whole youth-by-association thing. Mom actually looked surprised that there was a reason. Dad pursed his lips thoughtfully and nodded as if he hadn't thought of that either. Still, Mom wasn't ready to give in. She reached across the table and took my hand in hers. "Listen to me. There are some things you're still too young to understand. Ever since Hollywood began, movie stars have worked very hard to make people believe that they're all healthy, happy, and sober. But, as has been proven time and time again, that is very often not the case. Now, if you really believe that just because Aaron Ives *wants* you to report that Willow Twine is sober and stable means that she *really is* sober and stable, than this is worse than I thought, because they're trying to use you."

Now it was my turn to roll my eyes. "Gee, thanks, Mom. You really think I'm that stupid?"

"Of course I don't. But Willow Twine is an actress. And if it means saving her career, then I would imagine that it would be in her interest to put on her greatest performance ever."

"I have to agree with Jamie that doing that for an entire week would be pretty difficult," Dad said.

"And what if halfway through the week Jamie discovers that Willow Twine is sneaking into the closet every two hours to snort coke?" Mom asked. "Then what?"

"She calls a cab, goes to the airport, and catches the next plane home," Dad said.

"And there's Avy," I said.

"Your friend the runaway?" Mom scoffed. "Now that's a reassuring thought."

"That's so unfair!" I said. "His parents are totally supportive of what he's doing." What I didn't mention was the distance I felt growing between Avy and me. But I still believed that the next time we saw each other we'd pick up exactly where we'd left off as if we'd never stopped communicating at all.

Dad cleared his throat. "Do you realize that Jamie has stuck to her photography for almost three years? And in that time she's achieved things that many photographers never achieve in their entire lifetimes? Now, maybe it's still just a fad she'll someday outgrow—"

"Dad!" I gasped, feeling hurt by what he was implying.

He held up his hand. "Let me finish, honey. Maybe it's a fad, but maybe it isn't. None of us really knows. But what I do know is that, after all she's accomplished, it would be unfair of us to stop her from taking this assignment. Yes, for the first time in her life, she'll be far away and on her own. But she's been navigating around New York on her own for years. Frankly, that seems a lot more challenging than LA. I think she's probably ready for it." He turned to me. "We'll hear from you every day, right?"

"Hourly texts, if it makes you happy." I felt my spirits start to soar. This had to be the final volley of cannon fire that would win the war for my side.

In the den Alex made a sound that meant he wanted someone. Mom and Dad locked eyes for a moment. "I'll see what he wants," Dad said, and got up.

Mom waited until he left the room, then turned to me. I was surprised to see her eyes looking red rimmed and teary. She took my hand in hers. "Promise me you won't do the same thing?"

I gazed at her uncertainly. "What do you mean?"

"I mean, go out there and not come back. Like Avy."

The idea had never occurred to me. "No, Mom. No way. I promise."

A single tear spilled out of her eyes and ran down her cheek. "You're sure?"

"Yes, Mom. I promise. I swear."

DETECTIVE
CARLOS
RAMOS

01002 8.8 ISO AUTO

When people find out what I do, the first question they ask is, what famous people have I met? Have I met this one or that one? What was she like? Truth is, they're pretty much like everyone else. Some are nasty, some are nice. Some treat you like dirt. Some can't thank you enough for just doing your job. Big surprise, right?

When I get home at night, my wife and daughters know not to ask. They know I'll tell them if I met someone interesting or something happened that I think they'd like to hear about. But that doesn't stop them from reading all the magazines and watching all the TV shows. We'll sit at the dinner table and they'll talk about what this star did or that one said. I don't even know who they're talking about half the time because they only use first names. Like, "Did you see how much weight Rebecca gained?" And I'm like, "Rebecca who? We don't know any Rebeccas." And one of them will say, "Shut up and eat your dinner, Dad."

They talk about these famous people like they're our friends and neighbors. But maybe it's just natural. In the old days when we all lived in little villages, everybody saw everybody every day and knew everybody's business. So there was plenty to talk about. Now we go home at night and stare at the TV. Those are the people we see, so those are the ones we talk about, right? I mean, when you get right down to it, what's the difference between my wife and daughters arguing about some star's new diet and me and my friends arguing about Barry Bonds's home run record?

But I don't mean to say that things are the same as they've always been. When I was a kid and we talked about what we wanted to be when we grew up, we wanted to be things like firemen and astronauts and baseball players. Last week I read an article in *USA Today* where they asked kids what they wanted to be when they grew up. Eighty percent—four out of every five kids—said they wanted to be rich and famous. When did that become an occupation?

JAMIE

01002 8.8 ISO AUTO

THE NIGHT BEFORE I WAS TO LEAVE FOR LA FOR THE WILLOW ASSIGNMENT, Shelby had another party, but this time I didn't want to go.

"We'll just make an appearance," Nasim said on the phone when I told him I wanted it to be only the two of us that night.

"Do we *have* to?" I groaned.

"It would be impolite to accept the invitation and then not show up."

We agreed to meet at the party. Around ten thirty, the text came and I took a cab to a club in Chelsea. A woman in a dark coat standing at the door checked my name off a clipboard. The party was downstairs in a private room with a DJ playing loud dance music, a nonalcoholic bar, and a couple of waiters circulating through the crowd with trays of hors d'oeuvres.

I spotted Nasim talking to Shelby. Unlike most of the guys at the party, Nasim was wearing a blazer. The collar of his white shirt contrasted against his olive skin. I felt proud of how elegant he looked. While many of the girls wore jeans, Shelby wore a red dress.

"I'm so glad you could come," she said, kissing me on the cheek in a way that made me wonder if this was practice for the grand parties she would someday throw for her banker or lawyer or politician husband.

I turned to Nasim to kiss him hello, but somehow my lips hit his cheek and not his lips. While I was wearing jeans, I also had on my favorite fancy silk blouse and had been extra careful with my makeup and hair. I hoped he would notice and say something nice, but he didn't. Shelby went off to welcome her other guests. Feeling the music's loud, infectious beat, I slid my arms around Nasim's waist and began to sway.

He placed his hands on my shoulders, not around my waist, and said, "I thought you didn't want to come tonight."

It wasn't the most welcoming thing he could have said, but I decided to ignore it. "I'm happy as long as I'm with you." I kept swaying, hoping he'd slide his arms around me, but when I looked up at him, he was gazing off at the crowd. To get his attention, I said the first thing that came to mind: "I'm going to miss you."

"When do you leave?" he asked.

"Tomorrow morning."

"Shouldn't you be home, resting up for the trip?"

I stopped moving with the music and stared up at him, wondering why he'd said that. "Are you trying to get rid of me?"

"No," he answered without a smile or any other gesture to indicate that he found the thought silly.

"Are you sure?"

"Why would I want to get rid of you?"

"I don't know. Maybe because you think I've been a jerk with my obsession about being a celebrity photographer?"

"You know I think it's admirable," he said.

Was he being sincere or just saying what he thought I wanted to hear? And why wouldn't he put his arms around me? Was he afraid people might see? Ever since that afternoon when he'd been practicing piano and I'd taken the call from Carla, I felt like things had been different between us. As if Nasim had erected a wall where before there'd been a well-worn path. Feeling insecure, I pulled him closer. "You're not just saying that, are you?"

Waiting for his reassurance, I closed my eyes and pressed the side of my head against his shoulder. But when he didn't reply I opened my eyes and looked up at him. He was staring across the room . . . at Shelby.

A chill spread through me. Had I missed something major? Something between him and Shelby? Suddenly I didn't want to be at the party. "Can we go?"

Nasim scowled. "Where?"

"I don't care," I said, growing upset. "Anywhere. You said all we had to do was make an appearance."

"But where will we go?"

"I said I don't care. I just want to go." I know I sounded immature and bratty, but I was feeling unsure and scared and jealous. I didn't want him looking at Shelby. I wanted us to be alone, somewhere warm and cozy, secure in the knowledge that he was thinking of me and only me.

We wound up at a Starbucks with two cups of untouched tea on the small table between us. Nasim tapped a plastic stirrer against the tabletop.

"Is something going on with you and Shelby?" I asked.

He blinked and looked surprised. "No . . ."

"Are you sure?"

"I think I'd know. Why do you ask?"

"I don't know. The way you were both dressed tonight. And the way you looked at her. And the way you've been acting. I feel like you're still angry at me because I took that call from Carla at your house." I reached across the table and squeezed his hand. "I'm sorry I did that, really. I just . . . I don't know . . . ever since this whole photography thing started I feel like I've been so incredibly lucky, but I also feel like if I don't take advantage of this opportunity, I may never get a second chance. Sometimes it's really hard to know what's important and what's not."

I guess I was hoping that Nasim would squeeze my hand back, but he didn't. He stared down at the table, and I got the feeling there was something on his mind he was struggling with.

"What, Nasim?"

He pursed his lips. "You know, so much of our relationship is about you. And I know it's partly my fault because I just go along with it."

I didn't quite see it that way, but I knew if I argued, he would just withdraw into silence, so I tried, "You mean, like the photography?"

He nodded. "We spend so much time talking about you and what you are doing and what you are thinking about."

I told myself not to get defensive. Instead of letting it become an argument, I wanted to turn it into something positive. "I'd love to know more about what you're thinking," I said. "But you never want to talk about yourself."

"Yes, I know," he said. "So I think maybe I have to do more of that. It's just not something I'm used to."

I squeezed his hand again. "But you still like me, right? You're not going to dump me and fall in love with Shelby while I'm gone?"

He frowned. "Do you think you're just nervous about this trip?"

"Are you kidding? Not *just* nervous. Totally stressed. And I'd feel a lot better if I knew my boyfriend still cared about me."

His hold on my hand stayed firm. "I do."

"Are you *sure*?" I knew it wasn't cool to let all my insecurities spill out, but I really I needed to know the truth.

But instead of reassuring me again, Nasim stiffened and withdrew his hand. "I just told you I did."

Just when it felt like things were warming up between us, they went cold again. I could feel my emotions getting the better of me. "No, you didn't. All you've told me tonight was that I should go home and rest up for the trip."

"What's wrong with that?" he asked.

"I told you, I feel like you're trying to get rid of me. And I'm still wondering if it's because you'd rather be with Shelby."

Nasim glanced up at the ceiling as if he was getting impatient with my continued neediness. I felt stung by his insensitivity.

"I'm not up there," I snapped. "I'm here." I'd never snapped at him before and was as surprised as Nasim. I'd hardly ever snapped at *anyone* before. The harshness of my voice drew the attention of some of those seated around us. Nasim glanced at them, and then his eyes returned to mine. They were clear and direct, and maybe a little hard. He stood up. "I'll get you a cab."

"I can get my own cab," I said.

We went outside. I stood silently on the curb with my arms crossed while Nasim flagged a taxi. There was no way he'd let me get one on my own. He was much too much of a gentleman. And too much of a gentleman to get involved in a scene with his girlfriend in a Starbucks. Meanwhile, I tried to hold myself together on the outside, even though my insides were on wash cycle, churning and twisting.

A cab pulled up. Nasim held the door for me. I got in without saying good-bye and told the driver where to go.

And began to sob.

AVY

01002 8.8 ISO AUTO

NO OFFENSE, BUT TIJUANA IS A RINKY-DINK TOURIST-TRAP DUMP.
If it wasn't for all the wonderful and magical things they
offer on that side of the border, I'd never go near the
place. But it's almost like they know they don't have to
make the town nice to get you to come because this is
where you have to go to get what you can't get in the
States.

I wish my parents could see me sitting on this crowded
trolley. Their adorable, obedient Avy, who they expected
to go to all the best schools and become a lawyer and
marry a nice girl.

Meanwhile, Brad Cox, who took the role that was

supposed to be mine on *Rich and Poor*, is now starring in *Dave in Deep*, and I heard they've started offering him movie roles. That could have been me. That *should* have been me.

MY CALLS, E-MAILS, AND TEXTS WITH AVY CONTINUED TO SLOW. I TOLD myself we were both busy and involved in our own worlds, but to be honest, the whole cosmetic surgery thing really weirded me out. That wasn't the Avy I knew. Still, I was unhappy with myself for being judgmental. In early December I called him. After some superficial chitchat, he told me that he wasn't coming home for Christmas.

"Don't your parents want to see you?" I asked.

The phone line grew silent. I could hear a TV in the background. "I don't want to see them," he finally said.

"But they're sending you to the academy and paying

for you to live in a nice place and letting you do what you want to do."

Again there was quiet except for the TV. "Avy?" I said. "You there?"

"Did they tell you to call me?" he asked.

"Your parents?" The suggestion caught me totally by surprise. "No! I called because you're my friend and I care about you."

"You *sure* they had nothing to do with it?"

This was strange. It almost sounded as if he was being paranoid. "Avy . . . What a thing to ask. You're my best friend. What is this?"

"They've been giving me a lot of grief about Christmas," he said. "Saying the same exact things you just said. Like, 'We did everything you wanted us to do, so why won't you come home?'"

"Maybe that's what anybody would say. I mean, it *is* Christmas."

"Look, Jamie, I really don't want to talk about this, okay?"

I was shocked. We used to talk to each other about *everything*. "Okay, I guess."

The line was silent except for the TV in the background. I was tempted to make a crack that it seemed like he was more interested in what was on the tube than in me. Then he said, "I'll tell you what I'm doing over Christmas. But it really hurt me last time when you weren't supportive. You're my best friend, and I need to know you're behind me."

"Okay."

"I'm going back down to Tijuana."

I was careful not to react. "Uh, okay."

"Seriously, Jamie, I know what I'm doing."

"Uh-huh."

"God, Jamie, you sound like it is so *not* okay."

He was right, and I knew I had to be honest. I couldn't lie to him. He knew me too well. "I don't know what else to say, Avy. You know how I feel about it. I mean, what if I called you and said, 'Hi Avy, I have this big syringe of heroin, and I want to shove it into my arm and I need your approval.'"

"It is so totally not the same thing."

"I know, but we've always been honest with each other. Don't you want me to be honest with you now?"

"I always want you to be honest with me, Jamie, only you can't be honest if you don't know."

"Don't know what?" I asked.

"Just . . ." He hesitated. "What it's like. What I'm up against. It's different here. The rules, the attitudes. I told you, out here cosmetic surgery is like getting braces. Everyone does it. People would think it was weird if you *didn't* do it."

I believed him. It was practically impossible to look at a fanzine or website and not find ads promising fewer wrinkles and flatter stomachs. And was there a Hollywood star besides Diane Keaton who *hadn't* had cosmetic surgery? "I'm just not sure that means it's right for you. There's nothing wrong with your looks, Avy. And you've got something that's way more important than looks. You've got talent."

He laughed bitterly. "I have news for you, Wonder Girl. *Everyone* out here has talent."

E-MAIL TO
NASIM

01002 8.8 ISO AUTO

N,
I feel lonely and insecure when you
don't call or write. I know you don't
check your e-mail as much as most
people, but you must have read mine and
gotten my voice mail by now. Why no
replies?
   Anyway, I was sitting on the
guesthouse porch, watching the party
preparations--the caterer setting up
tables, the bartender stocking the
bar, the DJ and his sound system--

when Willow came across the lawn and sat down next to me. "You know what I'm going to say, don't you?"

I did.

"I'm really sorry about this," she said.

"You don't have to be."

"Yes, I do," she insisted. "I agreed to let you come all the way out here and document my life, and now I'm going back on my word. It's a really crappy thing to do. But"--she nodded toward Rex, who was chatting up the DJ--"you understand, don't you? After everything that's happened, we really can't let anyone know about this."

"Because of your contract with the studio?"

"No, it only says I have to stay clean. There's nothing in it that says I can't see him. But it really wouldn't go over well with my fans. It's a much better idea to wait until after the movie."

I understood and promised I wouldn't take any photos of them together or tell anyone. But you have to wonder about her judgment, N. I mean, she has to realize that getting together with Rex again could lead to something that could--potentially--destroy her career.

So, it's about eight o'clock now and the music's starting. Rex's guy friends are milling around, and there are some sketchy-looking girls here I haven't seen before. There's a weird vibe out there tonight, N.

Miss you tons and tons. Please write back or call! xoxoxoxoOXOXOXO

THE CAMERA FEELS HEAVY IN MY LAP. OR IS IT THE WEIGHT OF the shots in its memory? Shots that have the power to change people's lives forever. Willow's and mine, at least. From the other side of the door I hear Willow hiss, "No! Go away. Don't even talk to me. Just leave."

"You're not being fair." It's Rex!

"*I'm* not being fair?" Willow's words seethe with wrath. "Excuse me? After what you just told me?"

"But I didn't go through with it. I told you the truth. All you have to do is get the camera back. I can't believe how stupid I was. I'm sorry, Wills, really."

What's this? I wonder.

"You think all you have to do is say you're sorry? Are you out of your mind? Thanks to you, I could be five seconds away from seeing my entire career go down the toilet. You expect me to forgive you? You must be insane."

"No, Wills, I must be in love."

Why is it that sometimes the truest statements also sound the lamest? I'm tempted to pinch myself just to make sure this is real and that I haven't accidentally sleep-walked onto the set of a soap opera. But it's real all right. Only, why's she so furious at him?

"You're in love? That's why you took pictures of me without me knowing?"

Huh?

"If this is how you treat people you love," Willow snaps sarcastically, "I'd hate to see what you do to your enemies. You are so full of crap, Rex Dobro. Just go. Get out of my life and never come back."

I'm totally stunned. *Rex took the pictures on my camera? Why?*

"Look, I know you're angry, and you have every right to be. But I'm not walking away. Even if you truly never want to see me again, I'm not leaving you with this mess. I caused it, and I'm going to stay until it's straightened out."

"Want to straighten it out? Go find that little wench. Get that camera back and strangle her."

In the midst of my total bewilderment over what's

going on in the hall on the other side of the powder room door, it takes an extra second for the words to sink in. *Strangle her?* What's the saddest, bitterest, most pathetic and humiliating thought that can pass through anyone's mind at a moment like this? How about, *But I thought we were friends.*

Earth to Jamie. Wake up and smell the LA smog. You are not Willow Twine's friend. And you were a fool to think you ever were. You've been used, dimwit. People in this town don't have friends. They only have people they pretend to be friends with because they think they'll be useful to their careers. Did you really think you were the exception?

But I still don't understand what's going on. Why would Rex take those pictures? Why would he ever do something so terrible? Especially if he professes—and he sounded sincere to me—that he loves her? I stare at the angels on the pink powder room walls, and a single thought slowly takes shape in my mind: I can't wonder about that now. *First I need to get out of here.* Then I can figure out what's going on, and decide what to do with the photos.

But how do I get off this property when Willow's people are all out there looking for me? How will I get over that wall? Because I obviously can't stroll out the front gate.

I press my ear against the door but can't hear anything

in the hallway. My BlackBerry hasn't stopped vibrating, so I turn it off. My heart is banging. Should I really try to sneak out? Do I have a choice? I can't hide in here forever. Better go sooner rather than later, right? Better do it now, before Sam gets here with a private security SWAT team and starts dismantling the place.

I quietly open the door and peek out. No one's in the hall. There's no sound of movement nearby. Is this a trap? Are they lying in wait for me? I step out. Now what?

Footsteps start coming down the stairs. No time to think. I scoot into the kitchen, bracing for Maria to start screaming, but the kitchen's empty. I hurry out the back doors and around the pool toward the guesthouse.

And that's when I see the bright yellow ladder next to the tall hedges which hide the wall around the property.

I'm sprinting across the lawn. The gardener must have been trimming the hedges. I'm not good at judging heights, but I'd guess the wall must be twelve feet tall.

I drag the ladder through a thin gap in the hedge and prop it against the wall. Up close, it looks *really* high. I climb up, but even from the top of the ladder I still have to reach and pull myself up another two feet. For an instant I straddle the wall. It feels like sitting on a tree branch way up in the air, and between the tall palms and evergreens I can see the red tile roofs of the houses dotting the green Hollywood Hills. It's a long way down the other side of the wall, but I can't sit here and think about it. Anyone looking out of a rear window of Willow's house will see me.

I lower myself down the other side of the wall until I'm hanging by my fingertips, but it's still at least six feet to the ground below. What am I doing? If I let go and fall I'll break my leg! Terrified, I try to pull myself back up, but my hands aren't strong enough. My fingers are slowly sliding off the top of the wall, and I lose my grip.

I hit the ground and roll like they do in the movies. But it wasn't intentional. I only did it because I lost my balance. A moment later I'm sitting on the dirt staring at my feet. Amazingly, nothing hurts. I look back up at the wall and cannot believe I just climbed over it! When I have the time, I will have to congratulate myself on this insane act of bravery.

I get up and dust the dirt off. I'm surrounded by rubble. They're doing a teardown on this lot—dismantling an old house to build something new. Right now it's just a construction site—dirt, a gray concrete foundation, piles of debris, some yellow construction machinery, and big square pallets of bricks.

Oh, and one other thing. About two dozen yards away, some guy is standing on wooden scaffolding pressed against the wall. He has binoculars.

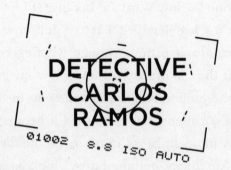

DETECTIVE CARLOS RAMOS

01002 8.8 ISO AUTO

We first heard about Richard Hildebrandt from Willow Twine's people. There'd been an incident at her place involving an unauthorized photographer, and a short time later Hildebrandt showed up at the front gate saying he was there to help. Twine's people told him to go away, and when he refused they apparently got a little rough with him.

Usually that's enough to get rid of a stalker, but in this case it appears to have confirmed what Hildebrandt was imagining—that Miss Twine was surrounded by dangerous people who might try to harm her.

Anyway, during this incident where Miss Twine's

people got rough with Hildebrandt, he made some statements that Doris Remlee, Miss Twine's assistant, picked up on. She went back through some old fan mail and e-mails and discovered that Hildebrandt had been writing to Miss Twine for several years. And some of what he wrote was pretty strange.

DAYS WILL PASS BEFORE YOU OPEN THE FEDEX BOX AGAIN. THIS TIME you will find a scrapbook. The first photo will bring new tears to your eyes. It's a shot of you and Avy sitting together at a school party in fourth grade. In front of you on paper plates are pink and blue cupcakes, each with a single candle.

On the next page is another photo of you and Avy, taken on the steps of the Metropolitan Museum of Art during the fall of freshman year. You and he were partners on a project about ancient Egypt, and you'd gone to the museum to see the mummies. You're wearing a bulky turtleneck sweater. Avy is wearing a hoodie. Your shoulders are pressed together, and you're grinning happily. You can't help thinking that this photo was taken less than two years ago and yet so much has changed. Back then you were just a couple of kids. You had school to attend, homework to do, parties you wished you'd been invited to, and favorite TV shows you always made sure to watch.

It wasn't that long ago.

But it feels so long ago, it's like ancient history.

On the next page are the shots you took of Tatiana Frazee in Cafazine. Why, you will wonder, would Avy put them in his scrapbook?

On the next page will be the *New York Weekly* story, THE YOUNGEST PAPARAZZO.

And on the next, the *New York Press* story: BABY PAP SCOOPS THE PROS AGAIN!

That's when you will realize this isn't a scrapbook Avy kept about himself. It's a scrapbook he kept . . . about you.

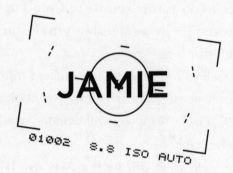

THE GUY WITH THE BINOCULARS CLIMBS DOWN FROM THE SCAFFOLDING
and starts toward me. He's wearing cutoffs, high olive-
colored military boots, and a green Army-surplus jacket
that looks much too warm for a day like today. His hair
is matted and disheveled, and his jaw is covered with
unshaved facial hair. And there's something wild and
strange about his eyes.

"Who are you?" he demands.

"Who are *you*?" I ask back, knowing the best defense
is often a good offense. "And what were you doing spying
on Willow Twine's property?"

Amazingly, my bluff seems to work. He's caught off

guard. "I," he stammers, "I have to protect her."

"From what?"

"People. You never know who. That's the problem."

A nervous shiver runs through me. He's a weirdo. I've seen enough of them on subways and New York City sidewalks to know the signs, but this is the first time I've encountered the Los Angeles variety. But this might be the good news.

"I think you're right," I tell him. "You have to protect her. You'd better stay here and make sure no one else comes over that wall."

His forehead creases and his eyebrows dip with consternation. "Is something wrong? Did something happen to her?"

"Not yet. But she's in danger. We need to be careful. Listen, if anyone asks, you didn't see me. You didn't see or talk to anyone. Understand? Just stay here and make sure no one else comes over that wall."

It's all nonsense, and I feel bad for feeding into his delusions, but this is an emergency. I make a wide circle around him and walk quickly toward the tree-lined sidewalk. A few minutes later, I get to a corner. Two women with blond ponytails and skintight Lycra tights are jogging in place, waiting for the light to change. Suddenly a car screeches around the corner. It's Sam, and he stares right at me.

TRANSCRIPT OF TESTIMONY

The State of California vs. Richard Curtis
Hildebrandt

DORIS ANNE REMLEE, being sworn to tell the truth,
the whole truth, and nothing but the truth tes-
tifies as follows:

My name is Doris Anne Remlee and I currently
reside at 41 Fairweather Court in the city of
Los Angeles. I was employed by Ms. Willow Twine
as her personal assistant. In that capacity it
was my responsibility to assist Ms. Twine in the
conduct of her professional and personal affairs.

Q: Did this include reading and answering correspondence?

A: Yes.

Q: And was this where you first became aware of the defendant?

A: Yes.

Q: Would you tell us about that?

A: Ms. Twine received dozens of fan letters every day. Many were addressed to her record company or film studio. A few were addressed to her agent or manager. It was rare for a fan letter to be addressed to her home. Ms. Twine preferred to keep her home address a secret. I first became aware of Mr. Hildebrandt because somehow he got Ms. Twine's home address and sent his letters directly to her there.

Q: Was that the only reason Mr. Hildebrandt's letters attracted your attention?

A: No. They were strange.

Q: Would you explain how?

A: Based on his letters, Mr. Hildebrandt seemed to feel that Ms. Twine was in danger and that he was the only one in the world who could protect her.

Q: Is that why you kept the letters?

A: Yes, I always kept the ones that sounded strange. There were lots of them from all sorts of people—vulgar, threatening, strange, and disgusting. I filed them away just in case. When I went back through the file I found about a dozen from Mr. Hildebrandt. They weren't particularly vulgar or disgusting. Not even that threatening. But they were definitely strange.

Q: Please tell us about the first time you saw Mr. Hildebrandt.

A: He came to the front gate of Ms. Twine's property. It was on a day that Ms. Twine was extremely upset because of some personal issues, and it was just by coincidence that a number of us were outside near the gate.

Q: Would you tell us who was there?

A: I was. And Zach Cushman, who did odd jobs around the house for Ms Twine. And Sam Russell, who was Ms. Twine's personal bodyguard.

Q: And what happened?

A: Mr. Hildebrandt came up to the gate wearing torn-off shorts and a green safari jacket with lots of cargo pockets. His hair was messy, and he had stubble on his jaw and chin. He said he had to speak to Ms. Twine. I told him she was away. That is our standard reply to strangers. Usually they would go away.

Q: Did Mr. Hildebrandt go away?

A: No. Mr. Hildebrandt replied that he knew

that was what we were supposed to say. He kept insisting it was important that he speak to Ms. Twine. He insisted that she knew him. He said it was urgent.

Q: Did he say why it was so important?

A: Yes. He said that her life was in danger.

Q: What happened next?

A: I told him that I would give any message he had to Ms. Twine when she returned. Then he asked me if my name was Doris.

Q: How would he know that?

A: I don't know. There had been a few stories about Ms. Twine in which my name was mentioned. He might have read one.

Q: Did he tell you why he thought her life was in danger?

A: He said Ms. Twine had to stop going around like she did, because there were people who wanted to harm her and he couldn't always be there to protect her.

Q: Did he explain what he meant by "going around"?

A: No, but I assumed he meant going shopping and out to restaurants and normal things like that.

Q: Would you tell us what happened next?

A: I told him again that I would give his

message to Ms. Twine when she returned and that it would be a good idea if he left.

Q: Did he?

A: No. He said that I didn't understand how great the danger was and that people were climbing over the wall around Ms. Twine's property and that for all I knew she might be in grave danger at that very moment. I told him that wasn't possible because she wasn't there.

Q: And what happened next?

A: He got excited and started to yell that I should stop lying and that he knew she was there and that it wouldn't be his fault if something terrible happened to her, because he couldn't be expected to stand guard there all the time.

Q: What happened next?

A: Sam Russell came over and told him to leave immediately. But Mr. Hildebrandt started yelling that Sam was incompetent and did a terrible job of protecting Ms. Twine and that anyone could just walk up on the street and stab her.

Q: He used those precise words?

A: Yes. He said anyone could just walk up and stab her. Sam again told him to go away, but Mr. Hildebrandt kept telling Sam what a bad job he was doing and how he, that is, Mr. Hildebrandt, would have done such a better job at protecting Ms. Twine.

Q: What happened next?

A: A car drove up. It was someone Ms. Twine wanted to see. We wanted to open the gate to let the car in, but we couldn't with Mr. Hildebrandt there. Sam asked him to leave again, but Mr. Hildebrandt became aggressive. He asked Sam if he knew who was in the car and why they were there. Then he said that if Sam wasn't going to search the car, he would. Well, of course, the people in the car had no idea what was going on or who Mr. Hildebrandt was. And that was when Sam went out and escorted Mr. Hildebrandt away.

Q: Can you tell us how he escorted Mr. Hildebrandt?

A: Mr. Hildebrandt refused to cooperate, so Sam had to twist his arm behind his back and walk him away.

Q: Mr. Hildebrandt has claimed that Mr. Russell assaulted him. Did you see anything that in your mind constituted an assault?

A: All I saw was Sam holding Mr. Hildebrandt's arm behind his back and escorting him down the road until they were out of sight. I didn't see anything that looked like assault.

JAMIE

01002   8.8 ISO AUTO

I'VE GOTTEN OVER THE WALL AROUND WIILLOW'S PROPERTY, PAST THE
weirdo, and am at the corner behind the blonde joggers
when Sam's car flies past and I could swear he looks
right at me. But the car keeps going, going . . . gone.

The light changes and the women jog across the street,
but I stand there, confused. It doesn't make sense. Sam
stared right at me. He had to have seen me.

Or maybe not. Was he distracted by the women in
their skintight Lycra? Was he just so fixated on getting to
Willow's that it didn't register?

Or did I just get incredibly lucky again? It doesn't
matter, I just have to keep moving.

Starwood, the showbiz-kids condo, is surrounded by lush green landscaping, towering palms, tennis courts, and swimming pools. I have to smile to myself. Only Avy could get himself set up in a place like this.

But when I ring the door of the apartment where he said he lived, a blond sevenish-year-old girl answers, and her mother tells me they've lived there for two months and don't know who lived there before them.

Moments later, in the condo office, I get Avy's forwarding address. His new place is in Inglewood, and the first three cab companies I call say they don't have any cabs available, which seems odd for the middle of a warm sunny day. The cabby who finally does take me says he'll drop me on a corner along West Manchester Boulevard but won't drive down any side streets. I get the feeling we're headed toward the wrong side of town.

"Why do you want to go there, anyway?" the cabby asks as he drives.

"I'm trying to find a friend."

He glances at me in the rearview mirror, and I have to believe he's thinking that I don't look like the kind of girl who'd have friends in Inglewood.

When I finally do find the two-story apartment building, it's scary run-down. Broken glass is scattered on the walkways. Tall, dry-looking brown weeds grow from the flowerbeds. About a foot of horrid green gunk sits at the bottom of the swimming pool.

I climb the cracked concrete steps to the second level. The door to room 239 is dented and scratched, as if someone once tried to kick it in. Instead of a curtain, a stained and torn green blanket covers the window. A rusty old air conditioner rumbles and drips water onto the walkway.

A television blares loudly inside. The doorbell doesn't work, so I knock. With all the noise from the television and a/c, it's difficult to hear, but through the door come sounds of hushed voices, clinking glass, and scurrying. "Just a minute!" a voice—not Avy's—calls.

More scurrying and hushed voices. Then someone calls out, "Who is it?"

"My name is Jamie. I'm a friend of Avy Tennent's."

The scurrying stops, but the hushed, unintelligible voices continue. A moment later the doorknob turns and the door opens a few inches. The apartment exhales sweet smoke and the stink of rancid garbage, and there's someone looking at me. His hair is dyed black and has that stiff, rigid look that overly processed and straightened hair gets. Skin so pale it's almost translucent, sunken eyes, a boy nearly emaciated in a stained baggy white T-shirt and dirty jeans. Behind him the dim apartment is lit by a three-bulb floor lamp, but only one bulb works. Two guys and a girl sit on a couch. The coffee table and floor are strewn with empty bottles, cans, takeout containers.

The guy in the doorway blinks in a way that makes me wonder when he last saw daylight. "Jamie?"

The voice sounds like Avy's and the eyes look familiar, but it's not the same nose. Like his face, it's much thinner. And the lips seem wrong, as if they're swollen unevenly.

"Don't you like it?" he asks.

Like what? Ohmygod! Suddenly I realize it *is* Avy. He's asking whether I like his new postsurgery "look." I'm in shock. He looks awful. "It's . . . uh . . . . Yes! . . . I'm just surprised. You're so . . . thin!" It's the only thing I can come up with that sounds remotely like a compliment. An overpowering urge to cry wells up inside me. *What has he done to himself?* I choke up and feel tears burst from my eyes.

"Jamie, what is it?" he asks.

"Avy," one of the guys grunts from inside the apartment, "close the damn door."

Avy steps out onto the walkway and pulls the door closed behind him. I cover my face with my hands and can't stop bawling. It's Avy, my best friend, but he's mutilated himself. I want to ask him why, but I can't.

"What's wrong, Wonder Girl?" he asks again.

My emotions are a totally disorganized jumble, a knot of different-colored threads. I'm on the run from Willow Twine. I don't know what's going on with Nasim back home, but I have a feeling it's bad. I've finally found Avy, but he's done something terrible to himself. If only I'd stayed in touch with him!

His skinny arms go around me. "You're just glad to see me and happy I'm okay, right?"

"Yes." I sniff and nod. If that's what he wants to believe, it's better than what I'm really thinking. I back away, dry my tears on my sleeve, force a smile. "It's so good to see you!"

"You, too!" He grins. One of his front teeth is chipped. When did that happen?

Next comes an awkward silence. I was planning to ask if I could stay with him just long enough to figure out what to do. But there's no way I'm staying in that smoky rat's nest.

Avy's grin fades, and the skin in the corners of his eyes creases uncertainly. "My parents didn't send you, did they?"

"I'm out here doing a story," I tell him. "I . . . wanted to see you."

"What kind of story?" he asks.

Even though I am seriously stressed and should probably be in a hurry to get out of town before Willow has the airport shut down, I feel like I can't leave my best friend like this. It's obvious that he's in bad shape. Suddenly what seemed like a huge problem in my life pales when compared with what appears to be going on in his.

His boney shoulders stick out under the T-shirt. He looks like he hasn't eaten in a month. "Avy, can I buy you breakfast?"

He frowns. "Sure. Only, it's almost dinnertime."

We walk down the block to a coffee shop. Avy's eyes dart left and right, and every dozen yards he abruptly jerks his head around and looks back over his shoulder. His movements are jittery and apprehensive. It's obvious he's worried about being seen or followed. But why would anyone be following us? Is this a real concern or just in his head?

I try not to stare at him, but I can't help glancing at his reflection in the windows we pass. *Avy, what have you done to yourself?* I want to ask. You used to be a cute guy. Now you look like a . . . I hate the word that keeps coming to mind because Avy is *not* a freak. He is my closest friend, someone I care about enormously.

I feel tears trying to creep into my eyes again. Oh, Avy, why? *Why!?*

"Crying again?" he asks in the middle of lighting a cigarette.

"No, it's just this smog. Doesn't it burn your eyes?"

"You get used to it," he says, exhaling a plume of smoke.

Back in New York, he never smoked. He said it was a gross, disgusting habit. Forget the health issues. It stained your fingers and teeth and made your clothes stink. That was reason enough not to do it.

In the coffee shop Avy doesn't want to sit near the windows. I don't know if it's because it's too bright or he's worried someone passing by might see him. Or maybe he's self-conscious about his new appearance? Whatever the reason, we sit in the back, in the shadows. Avy's a mess of jitters and tics. The fingers of his right hand are yellow with nicotine, and his fingernails have been chewed into stubs. *What's happened to him?*

The waitress pours coffee. Avy dumps a ton of milk and sugar in his. His hands tremble, and some of the sugar misses the cup and spills onto the table. I'm trying to think of something to say that won't sound totally lame, but it's difficult to collect my thoughts, because I'm still on the verge of bursting into tears.

"So, you're here doing a story?" he asks.

I tell him briefly about my assignment to cover Willow but say nothing, of course, about the most recent developments.

"A week with Willow Twine?" Avy's mouth drops open in awe. "That's amazing!"

Still trying to recover from what happened at her place earlier today, all I can do is shrug. Avy smirks and offers his own interpretation of the gesture. "Yeah, not so amazing for you, Wonder Girl. The photo prodigy, right? Just the same old same old. But seriously, Jamie, you really hung with her? Partied with her? Stayed in her mansion? That's *incredible!*"

Oh, Avy, if only you knew what I know! But I have to be cool. "It's a job, Avy. She wanted something from me, and

I wanted something from her. I guess you could say we had a deal. That's all it was."

But even as the words leave my lips, I'm wondering how I could have been such a fool to think Willow and I had become friends? How could I have believed even for a second that it was anything other than business? And again, why would Rex take those photos? And what role am I playing in this crazy mystery?

"Yeah, but think about it, Wonder Girl. You and Willow Twine had a deal going. How many people can say that?" For a second it's the old Avy. Filled with envy and eager excitement whenever I talked about coming into contact with someone famous. But then his forehead creases. He takes an e-cig out of his pocket. Is he so addicted to smoking now that he can't even sit in a coffee shop for half an hour without doing it? He inhales, leans back in the booth, and stares at the glowing red tip. I know him well enough to sense something's bothering him.

"What is it?" I ask, nervously fingering my coffee cup.

"You could've helped me, Jamie."

"I did."

Avy shakes his head. "All you did was give me Carla's number. She gave me names of two talent agencies I probably could have looked up myself, and after that never returned a phone call. You could've done more. I mean, you're supposed to be my friend. With all the famous celebrities you've met, you couldn't once have said, 'Hey, I have a really talented friend. Maybe you could use him in your next TV show or movie or commercial'?"

That stings. "It doesn't work that way, Avy. I wasn't in a position to ask those people for favors. They're already doing *me* a favor by letting me take their picture. I mean, seriously, you think they care who takes their picture? Today it's Jamie Gordon. Tomorrow it could be Davy Axelrod, or any of a thousand other photographers or videographers. And the one sure way for me to guarantee that it won't be me tomorrow is if I do something to get on their nerves."

"But you just spent *a week* with Willow Twine. You couldn't have mentioned me or asked her to invite me over?"

"I tried your old number and it didn't work, Avy. I went to the address you gave me and they said you'd moved long ago. I've been texting you all week and you never hit me back." But I could have looked for Avy sooner during this trip. There had been more than enough downtime to do that.

Avy gazes sadly at me as if he knows I'm not being entirely sincere. "I e-mailed you all that information months ago. The change of address. My new cell phone number. I guess it was just one of the e-mails I sent that you never bothered to read."

I stare down at my coffee. It's true. There were some

e-mails I didn't answer. I was just so upset about his cosmetic-surgery plans. "But I sent you e-mails you never answered, either."

"Not true," Avy replies. "I answered every one I could, Jamie. If I didn't answer a few, it was because I was away."

"Away?"

Avy rubs the side of his thin new nose thoughtfully, as if he's trying to make up his mind about something. "Mexico mostly." He gestures to his face. "So, you still haven't told me what you think."

I'd been afraid he would ask. "It's so different, Avy. It's going to take me some time to get used to."

His new face falls. "You don't like it."

"I didn't say I didn't like it. You know you look different."

Now it's Avy's eyes that start to get watery. He wipes the tears away with his fingers, and I feel awful and guilty for not being a better friend. He came out here all by himself. It must have been so lonely. I reach across the table and take his hand. "You're right, Avy. You deserved better from me. I'm sorry. I really am."

Avy nods, sniffs, wipes away a tear with the heel of his hand, gazes off. "I don't know, maybe it wouldn't have helped, anyway. It's not like I haven't been hustling, auditioning, doing everything I can to get noticed. Everything! I mean, Jamie, I did things . . . things I can't even talk about." Fresh tears appear, and he dabs them with a napkin. "I don't get it. I mean, I know I'm good. You know I'm good. Back in New York, at Herrin, I was the most talented actor they'd ever seen. Everyone said so. I got those commercials. I would have had that role on *Rich and Poor* if my stupid parents had let me."

"Avy, you *are* talented. Seriously, I can't believe that in all this time you haven't gotten a single gig."

"I've had a few, but mostly dead-end, pathetic, non-speaking parts. Extras work. Crap that never led anywhere. You have no idea how hard it is out here, Jamie. How many other Avy Tennents there are fighting for the same roles. Out here I'm not one *in* a million. I'm one *of* a million. It sucks, Jamie. It really does. You just have no idea."

I squeeze his hand. "But if this is what you really want to do, you have to keep trying. I'll be more supportive. I'll never let you down again. From now on I'll always, *always* be there for you. I promise."

He smiles weakly and gazes off in thought.

"So . . . are you still auditioning?" I ask. I know what I saw back at that apartment. But he must be trying to do *something*.

Avy shakes his head. "I'm taking a break. Trying to do some writing. Movie scripts, TV pilots, stuff like that. I've got a friend who knows Seth Stieg. He's Tim Stieg's brother. Remember that Bravo series about the last woman on Earth? That was Tim's show. Seth says Tim's looking for some new ideas. So, Dan and I are trying to come up with stuff."

"Was Dan one of the people back at the apartment?" I ask.

Avy frowns, then nods. He stares at his e-cig as if suddenly fascinated. "Yeah, I know. Not the most productive atmosphere, huh?"

"Why did you leave the condo in Starwood?"

He shrugs. "They treat you like a kid. You're constantly chaperoned. I didn't come all the way out here to have a curfew, you know? Never had one back home. Why do I need one here? I can make it out here on my own, Jamie. I just need a break."

I believe him. Only, who's going to give this trembling, nicotine-stained, surgically altered semi–basket case a break? I can't help thinking that the only roles he looks ready for are a drug fiend or a zombie.

Then he gives me that impish look I remember so well from Herrin. It's almost a relief. Like there's still a little of the old Avy left. "So, maybe Dan and I move a little product on the side. It pays the rent, and it's no big deal, Jamie. Everybody in this town uses. I swear, it's just like on *Entourage*. Everyone does a little something. And the crazy thing is, it's considered a legitimate way up. I mean, from dealing into acting. You wouldn't believe how many stars and people high up in the business started out peddling bags and grams. Some really famous people . . . including Willow's old boyfriend."

"Rex?" I blurt. Of course, like most of the world, Avy doesn't know that Willow and Rex have just gotten back together. Although, from the way things sounded when I left, it's a pretty good bet they won't be together much longer.

Avy smirks. "How do you think Dobro supported himself all those years while he tried to get bands going? They used to call him drug dealer to the stars."

RICHARD

01002 8.8 ISO AUTO

Dear Willow,
   I am very angry that you have
not called or written me back. You
know how I feel. Dont you care?
Everyone else takes from you. I only
want to give. You dont want to be
sorry someday do you?
   And next time I see that big bald
head jerk that works for you he
better watch out. I will cut him up
so bad like sliced salami.
   Did the police tell you I talked to

them? I told them about the danger
you are in. I think they understand
but how much can they do when this
whole city is full with creeps and
criminals and sick people? Can they
give you protection 24/7 like you
need? I dont think so.

I wonder if maybe you dont believe
you are in danger. Or maybe those
stupid people like the big bald head
jerk and Doris tell you there is no
danger because they know they cant
protect you and dont want to lose
their job.

You need to have me protect you
because I am the only one that loves
you. Do I have to show you how much
danger you are in? Do I need to show
you how much you need my protection?

You know who I am. You should
answer me. We dont have forever. I
can feel that the danger is getting
closer. Please answer me. Please let me
protect you from him before it is too
late.

I love you.
Richard

"SO, HOW ARE THINGS WITH NASIM?" AVY ASKS IN THE COFFEE SHOP.

"Okay," I manage.

He gives me a look. "That didn't sound encouraging."

All I can do is shrug. Avy has enough problems and doesn't need to hear about mine, so I make up a lame excuse to avoid talking about Nasim and change the subject. "It's just hard being so far away. Don't you want something to eat?"

"Naw. Not hungry."

That's hard to believe, considering how scrawny he is. We finish our coffees. Through the windows the California sun is going down and the sky is blue, purple, pink, and orange. The red-eyes will start to takeoff for the east coast in a few hours. I know I should get moving, although I hate leaving Avy like this. "I'm going back to New York tonight. Why don't you come with me?"

He slumps in his seat and gazes up at the ceiling. That momentary impishness, that glimpse of the old Avy, disappears. "So everyone can see what a failure I am? So they can see that I didn't make it?"

"They won't care. Just come back with me, okay? This isn't the right place for you, Avy. These are the wrong people. You need a fresh start. Please? You don't have to go to your parents' if you don't want to. We'll move in with my father. He's got room. You can be my roommate. We'll get you cleaned up and healthy. You can look for acting jobs in New York, and maybe after a while you can come back out here and start fresh."

Avy looks across the table at me, and his eyes are soft and sad. He takes a drag off the e-cig and exhales thin vapor. "You mean it, Jamie?"

"Of course I mean it."

A crooked smile creases his lips. "Maybe I should."

Inside of me a warm bud of hope blossoms. In the middle of everything that's gone wrong, maybe this is one thing I can make go right. "Great! We'll fly back tonight. I'll put your ticket on my debit card. You can pay me back when you get the money."

"Yeah." Avy nods. "Only, I can't go back tonight.

There's one thing I have to do first. It'll just take a few weeks."

The blossom begins to wilt. "Are you sure?"

"Yeah. It's just this one thing."

The fact that he won't say what it is worries me. "Can't you do it when you get back to New York?"

"No. It's something . . . I have to do here, Jamie. I promise I'll come back as soon as it's over. Really, I will."

"In a few weeks?"

"A month, maybe. Not more than that. I promise." He's drumming his fingers, glancing at the coffee shop door.

A month? What could possibly take a month? "Are you sure, Avy? Why not come back with me tonight? We'll start all over together. You and me. Just like—" I was going to say "old times," but it won't be. I'm not sure what it will be like for Avy back in New York. I can only hope it will be better than it is here.

He wraps his arms around himself, tucks his hands into his armpits as if the temperature has suddenly dropped. I hear tapping and realize it's his foot. He takes another puff on his e-cig, then flicks away an imaginary ash with jittery fingers.

"I'm worried that you'll change your mind," I tell him honestly.

"I won't, Jamie. I promise. I'll just take care of this one thing and then I'll come." He places his hands on the table and gives me a nod. It's time to go.

Out on the sidewalk, Avy spreads his arms for a good-bye hug. I step close and slide my arms around his skinny, bony body.

"Promise me one more time you'll come home," I whisper.

"I promise," he says, but he's already pulling out of my grasp.

Filled with a sense of foreboding, I grab his shirt and stop him. "Swear?"

"Swear." He grins and winks. Then, once again, like that hot summer night back in New York City the previous August, he strides away down the sidewalk.

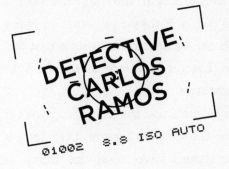

DETECTIVE CARLOS RAMOS

01002   8.8 ISO AUTO

We have to tread a very fine line in some of these cases. Especially where there's been no outright threat. Richard Hildebrandt hadn't said or written anything threatening to Willow Twine. This was a case where the only person who'd suffered any harm was Richard Hildebrandt himself. If he'd walked into any LAPD station after Sam Russell roughed him up and had shown the police his bruises, I think the police would have been obligated to bring Russell in and book him for assault. It wasn't like Hildebrandt had been trespassing. He'd been on the street. I guess we're just lucky that some of these creeps and weirdos don't realize that the law is there to protect their rights, too.

Anyway, at that point we knew we had to do something. LA is a funny place. A real company town. Only ten percent of the people who live here actually work in show business, but they're what keep the rest of this place going. If they ever start to leave, this town is finished. So we had to make sure that Ms. Twine felt protected, even if it was from someone who had not broken any laws.

In this kind of case the only thing we can do is find out where the person lives and go have a chat with him. You should have seen the dump Hildebrandt lived in. One of those welfare motels with broken windows and weeds growing everywhere. You see these places and you really have to wonder why the Health Department allows them to operate. We waited until Hildebrandt came out, and then we strolled up to him and flashed our badges. He immediately got defensive, like, "What did I do? I haven't done nothin'."

"We know that," we told him. "We just want to talk."

"What about?" he asked.

"Willow Twine."

That took some of the wind out of his sails. I guess he realized we knew. Sometimes that's all it takes. They know the jig is up. But not this guy. Suddenly, in his mind, we were all on the same team.

"Can you help her?" he asked.

"How?" we asked.

He actually looked astonished that we didn't already know. "She's in danger."

"Why?" we asked.

"Every time she goes out in public, there's nobody to protect her."

"She's got a bodyguard," we reminded him.

"He's useless!" Hildebrandt started to get upset. "Anyone could get past him and shove a knife in her chest."

"Why would anyone want to do that?"

He looked at us like we were stupid. Like the answer was totally obvious. "Because she's Willow Twine."

I remember sharing a look with my partner at that point, like, *Whoa, we've got a real freak show here.* But at the same time, I got an idea of how we could spin this to our advantage. I said, "Okay, thank you. I'm glad you told us about this. You're completely right. A star of Willow Twine's magnitude should have more protection. We are definitely going to speak to her people. My guess is that she's really going to appreciate you for this."

It seemed to work. Hildebrandt seemed satisfied with that. He even thanked us. I thought, *Well, that was easier than I expected.* To be honest, it was as much as we could do under the circumstances. And even then we were probably stretching the rules a little.

You know, you try to do the right thing. That's why you're in this business. And I think most of the time things do work out for the best. But once in a while, something goes completely haywire. And then you ask yourself, what could I have done differently? How could I have avoided this tragedy? I've asked myself that a lot in this case. And to be totally honest, I can't think of a thing.

IT FEELS WRONG TO LEAVE AVY, BUT I HAVE TO GET OUT OF LA BEFORE
Willow tracks me down. Everybody flies in and out of
LAX. I bet a lot of stars have never even heard of the
airport in Ontario, California, so that's where I take the
cab. From the back of the cab, I call Dad.

"Hey, honey, what's up?" he asks.

"Get me on a flight home from Ontario airport ASAP.
I don't care how many connections I have to make."

"What's going on? Is something wrong?"

"Get me on a plane and call me back. I'll explain
then."

"Will do." One thing I can say about Dad—when I

need him to come through, no questions asked, he does it. What a sweetheart.

Meanwhile, now that I've turned my BlackBerry back on I can see that there are dozens of calls and text messages, mostly from Carla and various editors in New York, but also from Doris Remlee, Willow, and someone named Charles DuPont from the LA law firm of Ballard, Harris, and Schmidt. It's not hard to guess that they want to threaten me with some kind of legal action if I don't turn over my camera.

Dad couldn't get me on a direct flight back to New York, so I had to catch a red-eye to Atlanta, and then an early-morning flight to New York. When I finally trudge, bleary-eyed from lack of sleep, out of the terminal at LaGuardia, Dad's waiting in his car. I lean across the front seat and kiss him on the cheek. "Thanks, you're the best."

"Where's your stuff?" he asks as he starts to drive.

"Had to leave it."

He scowls at me. I tell him the whole story while he drives back to the city.

"I don't get it," he says when I've finished. "Why would Rex take those pictures?"

"Don't have a clue, Dad. Can't figure it out. Was he high? Was he just goofing around, planning to erase them, but then he forgot? He had to know the danger to Willow's career. Nothing really makes sense."

"So, you've really got Willow's future in the palm of your hands," Dad says. "And you can probably make big money by selling these pics . . . I mean, didn't Brangelina's baby photos sell for something like fourteen million dollars?"

"Yes, but not these," I answer. "Everyone seems to think I've got shots of Rex and Willow, but that's not what I have. They're just of Willow. It's huge news, but it's negative news. The big media outlets don't pay a lot for negative news. *People* magazine would never run these photos. It's kind of weird. They know their audience wants to know about stuff like this but doesn't want to actually see it. They'll pay tons for weddings and pregnancies and new-relationship shots. But what I've got really isn't photos. It's a story. The photos just prove the story is true. No one feels really proud about taking someone like Willow down. You can't feel good about destroying someone's career. It's not like she's a bad person. It's almost like she's a sad person."

Dad nods slowly and we drive off the Fifty-ninth Street Bridge and ease into Manhattan traffic—yellow cabs and big white buses with lots of dark windows. "I'm impressed by how well you understand how these things work," Dad says. "I guess the thing I don't understand is, if you can't make much money from the photos and you feel so bad about hurting Willow's career, why not just erase them?"

That's the big question. And I guess he's the one person

I can admit the truth to. "Because . . . it could be a really huge boost for my career."

The words hang between us in the car. Then Dad says, "But you already *have* a career. Suppose you destroy the photos? You've still come back from a week shooting Willow Twine. It's an exclusive, and it's all yours."

Yes, I think, a nice feather in my cap, but nothing that would really change anything. How can I explain to him what I'm feeling? "Dad, remember the night you got us in to Club Gaia? You couldn't have done that if I hadn't been in *New York Weekly*."

His brow furrows as he drives. "Right, but . . . so what?"

"So what?" I repeat, astonished. "Don't you want to get in to Club Gaia again?"

Dad glances at me, and I think I can read in his expression that now he understands. "Seriously? What difference does it make? The only reason I wanted to go there was to see if the story had enough juice to get us in. It was a lark. Just a goof."

I'm not sure I believe him. "So . . . you're saying you don't really care if you never get in to Club Gaia again?"

He chuckles. "Come on, honey. I don't hang out in places like that."

I'm still not sure I buy that. "No offense, Dad, but you're such a groupie," I tell him, half-teasing, but half-serious. "Like, you always know who all the stars are."

"And your point is?"

The car bumps over a manhole cover. I hear what he says, and I also hear what's left unsaid: *Being able to identify stars doesn't mean you want to be one. Being able to get in to a club shouldn't define who you are. You should already know who you are.*

But maybe I'm just finding out.

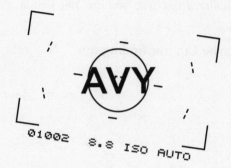

CAN'T TELL YOU HOW GLAD I AM TO GET OFF THAT FREEZING COLD trolley and step into the hot sunshine. I go through the turnstile with the day-trippers, college kids, and maids and walk along the wall with the big mural that leads into Tijuana.

A few blocks off the main drag is a whole different world. Shanties with corrugated-metal roofs, unpaved dirt streets with foul-smelling rivulets of water running down them, barefoot kids in tattered shorts and stained T-shirts, groups of nasty-looking hombres hanging around in the shadows of doorways. It's in a kitchen behind a small taco stand that I can finally strip off my girdle of tape and money and hand it over to a short man with greasy black hair and a thick scar under his lower lip. Now I'm free to check in to Dr. Varga's clinic. When I get out in three weeks, I'll come back to this taco stand and pick up the goods I'm taking back to San Diego.

By the way, just because I've come to Tijuana for my surgery doesn't mean Dr. Varga is some crackpot performing operations on his kitchen table. In the good doctor's office is a framed diploma from the Albert Einstein College of Medicine in New York City, one of the best medical schools in the United States. His clinic glistens with cleanliness, and everything is new, computerized, and first-rate. The only reason cosmetic surgery is so much cheaper on this side of the border is that doctors don't have to pay the huge cost of malpractice insurance that doctors in the United States have. But in terms of botched surgeries, you're just as likely to have one north of the border as you are here.

DAD KEEPS HIS CAR IN A GARAGE A FEW BLOCKS FROM HIS building. We're walking along the sidewalk when a flash unexpectedly goes off in our faces. It's quickly followed by another and another. The paparazzi have come out of nowhere—a crowd of them on the sidewalk in front of us. But why are they taking photos of my father and me?

"What happened with Willow?"

"Is it true that you stole something from her?"

"We heard you guys were good friends."

"You trying to give the paparazzi a bad name?"

"What are you talking about? She's not paparazzi. She's a celebrity photographer!"

The strobes flash, and the video lights are blinding. My eyes are so blitzed by blazing illumination that I can hardly see. I raise my hand—a natural reaction to block the intense glare, but also a shot the paparazzi loves. A raised hand shouts, *Leave me alone!* and *I don't want my photo taken!* and *I'm guilty!*

Dad shields his eyes too, and we keep walking while the paparazzi swarm. It's so strange, because I know, or at least recognize, so many of them.

"What's the matter, Jamie? Can't talk?"

"Think you're too good for us now?"

They're right. What am I doing? Even though I know I'm not supposed to stop, I have to. These are the people I work with, and now that I'm back in New York I'll be spending a lot of time with them. At least, I hope I will. The strobes keep flashing; the shutters are a din of clicking. I concentrate on appearing relaxed and open. "Seriously, guys? I haven't taken anything from anyone. I really don't understand what's going on with Willow. I'm just a photographer like the rest of you. I have a feeling you've gotten some bad information."

My old pal Davy steps forward out of the silhouettes and flashing lights. "Come on, Jamie, that's BS and you know it."

More strobes flash, but the group quiets as if they're waiting to hear how I respond. "All I can tell you is that I didn't take anything from Willow Twine. And I don't know what's going on."

Both of these statements are true. The photos belong to me, and I don't know why Rex took them.

"They're saying you climbed a wall to get off Willow's property," someone says.

The answer to that one comes so quickly it surprises me. "The wall around Willow's house must be twelve feet tall," I reply. "Look at me. You really think I could climb something like that?"

A couple of the paparazzi chuckle as if they realize how ridiculous the idea is, even though that's exactly what I did do. The cameras stop flashing.

"I'm sorry, guys, really," I tell them. "I hate to have to tell you that you're wasting your time. I'm not the news. I'm just one of you."

Looking disappointed, they lower their cameras and switch off their video equipment. The crowd starts to disperse. Davy lingers behind the others, waiting until they're gone. When it's just my dad, him, and me, he asks, "So, how was it? I mean, hanging out with Willow for a week?"

"A real eye-opener," I answer.

Davy gives me an arch look, as if he's smart enough to know how many different meanings that answer could have. I step a little closer and lower my voice. "I promise I'll tell you the whole story when I can, okay? But I'm not news. I'm really not."

"Okay, kid," he says. "And well, anyway, welcome back."

New York Times

HOLLYWOOD STARLET STABBED TO DEATH

Willow Twine, the actress, singer, and idol to millions of pre-teen girls, died from stab wounds this afternoon inflicted by an apparently deranged man who accosted her on the sidewalk outside a popular Rodeo Drive eatery.

Police said Ms. Twine, whose real name is Jane Ellen Hutter, had just left Encore Django when she was approached by the man, tentatively identified as Richard C. Hildebrandt, who thrust a nine-inch knife into her chest. Hildebrandt was quickly subdued by Ms. Twine's bodyguard, and police were called, but an EMT who was on the scene said later that the actress expired before the ambulance arrived.

"There was massive internal bleeding," said the EMT, who

asked not to be identified because he was not authorized to speak on the record. "If I had to guess, I'd say that the knife must've severed her aorta."

A spokesperson at Cedars-Sinai Medical Center would say only that despite emergency surgery, Ms. Twine could not be revived.

Word of Ms. Twine's untimely death spread quickly on Twitter, with several websites reporting the news within minutes. Tearful, heartbroken fans soon began to gather at the restaurant with flowers, framed photos, notes of tribute, and candles for the young actress. Most expressed shock and dismay that anyone would want to harm the young woman. . . .

San Diego Union-Tribune

UNIDENTIFIED TEEN DIES IN HOSPITAL

Mexican authorities reported today that an unidentified male teenager died yesterday at General Hospital in Tijuana as a result of what doctors said was botched plastic surgery performed at an unlicensed cosmetic-surgery clinic.

Authorities believe the victim, whose age was estimated at between fifteen and eighteen, is an American. They are asking the public for help identifying him.

Doctors reported that the victim was brought to the hospital emergency room by an unknown person who told a nurse the man had gone to the Tijuana clinic for calf implants. The person then fled before police could question him.

Doctors said the victim died from gangrene caused by a massive infection. No identification was found on the body, and no further information was available.

JAMIE

0100Ƨ 8.8 ISO AUTO

YOU LEARNED OF WILLOW'S DEATH WITHIN MINUTES OF IT HAPPENING. But it will be weeks before Avy's parents report him missing, and another month will pass before he is identified as the nameless young man who died of an infection in a Tijuana hospital.

The news of Willow's murder was broadcast, tweeted, blogged, and printed everywhere. Fans around the world held candlelight memorials. Dozens of video elegies sprang up on YouTube. Movie stars, politicians, and others were quick to grab the spotlight to bemoan her passing.

The news of Avy's death will come in a phone call from a friend of Mr. and Mrs. Tennent's. She will tell you that Mrs. Tennent would like you to attend her son's funeral.

You will see Nasim at the service. Back in late March, when you returned to school after spring break, numerous "friends" were eager to tell you that Nasim had started seeing Shelby Winston. And then Nasim confirmed it. Of course you were hurt, but, to be honest, by that point not completely surprised. It wasn't only because he'd sent one short e-mail over spring vacation. Really, you'd sensed for a long time that you were losing him, and even while you tried to patch things up, you were preparing yourself for the worst, especially after you got the feeling something might be up with Shelby.

I mean, is it completely bent to think that at least it's Shelby you lost to and not some "lesser" female? And, while it would have been much better to have heard about Shelby from Nasim himself rather than from other people, what's done is done. You will feel hurt and angry, but deep down you also know you have to blame yourself as well. Like Nasim intimated the night before you left for LA, maybe if you hadn't been so obsessed with your career, things would be different.

Except for a few of Avy's cousins, you and Nasim will be the only young people at the funeral. Even though Avy and Nasim were friendly, they were never really good friends, and seeing Nasim at the service will both sting and remind you that he is a good person, the kind of person who will come to a funeral even when his presence is not expected. School has ended for the summer, and many of your classmates will be off to summer homes, or on teen tours or family trips to faraway places. Most of the small crowd at the church will be family and friends of Mr. and Mrs. Tennent's. You will wonder how many of them really knew Avy.

You and Nasim will not sit together, but after the ceremony you will find yourselves standing near each other on the sidewalk, watching as family members get into black limousines to follow the hearse to the cemetery. The burial itself will be private, for close relatives only, so you will be spared falling apart when that polished dark brown mahogany coffin is lowered into the earth.

The hearse and limos will pull away and meld into the traffic, leaving you and Nasim on the sidewalk. It will be the first time you will be face-to-face since he told you he was seeing Shelby, and you'll be filled with turmoil and contradictory emotions. You'll want to tell him how angry and embarrassed you were at having to hear about Shelby from others, and at the same time you will be tempted to suggest getting a cup of coffee and catching up, yearning, really, to tell him how much you miss him. But will be too late for that.

"How are you?" Nasim will ask.

You will shrug. What will there be to say, really? About Avy? About you? It's all changed.

"And you?" you will ask.

He'll hang his head and look down. "I'm . . . sorry for

the way things turned out, and that you heard from others before I had a chance to tell you myself."

Your insides will wrench. *Yes,* you will think, that is exactly what you wanted to hear, only now that he's told you, it only makes the hurt of losing him worse. *Such a handsome, honest, charming guy.* So straightforward and unpretentious. You will feel a catch in your throat. "I really have to go. See you."

You will hurry away down the sidewalk, glad he can't see the tears running down your face.

AFTERWORD

`01002  8.8 ISO AUTO`

"I'LL TELL YOU WHAT I FOUND OUT," CARLA SAID. "BUT YOU HAVE TO swear you won't repeat it to anyone."

We were in her office. It was early evening and the phone had stopped ringing. Outside it was still daylight. The days were growing longer.

She exhaled a plume of smoke into the air. "It was a setup. Aaron Ives was behind it. He wanted those photos out there for the world to see."

This makes less than no sense to me. Willow was Ives's biggest client. She was his meal ticket, and probably the only reason he ever got to be as powerful as he was. Had those photos come out, Willow would have violated her contract with the movie company. She would have been tossed from *The Pretenders*. It would have been the end of her career and Aaron's as well.

Carla saw the confusion on my face. "Aaron was through with her. He knew she was finished."

"But she had *The Pretenders*."

"It wasn't enough to salvage her career. If the movie was a hit, it might have prolonged things for six months or a year, but basically she was done. Too old for the kids. They're ready for someone new. And I don't have to tell you who that is."

Everyone knows Alicia Howard took over Willow's role in *The Pretenders*.

"But even if that's true, it still doesn't explain why Aaron wanted to short-circuit Willow's career," I point out.

Carla gazed at me with a knowing smile. "What does Alicia Howard want more than anything in the world?"

That gave me pause. "A platinum album? An instantly sold out music tour? A top-rated TV show?"

Carla raised an eyebrow, as if to say, *What else?*

Then it hit me. "*The Pretenders?* You mean, Alicia wanted the role, and Aaron Ives needed a new superstar to replace Willow . . ."

Carla nodded. "It was simple. If he could get Alicia the role, she would sign him as her manager."

I'm stunned into breathessness. The manipulation . . . the heartlessness . . . the cruelty of it . . . And to think that I was so worried about hurting Willow's career for my own advancement, when Aaron Ives probably never thought twice about sabotaging her so he could sign Alicia.

"No, not unbelievable," said Carla. "Just another day in show business."

But there was something else. "Why would Rex—"

Carla chuckled devilishly. "It's funny how everyone thinks that just because you get to be a famous rock star for a while that you must be rich. But it's amazing how fast you can burn through five or ten million. Rexy bought the dream. The big house, the hot cars, diamond baubles for his best girls, the drugs and other party favors for himself and his entourage. And, of course, he never expected to get hit with two major lawsuits for unfinished albums. But before he knew it, not only was he broke, he was a couple of million in debt."

My insides twist at the implications. "And that's when Aaron Ives came into the picture?"

Carla nodded. "I imagine that in return for those photos, Rex's legal problems would have been resolved, a new band would have been formed, and a concert tour planned. He'd be a rock star again instead of a has-been." She toyed for a moment with her pen, then gazed searchingly at me. "There's only one thing I don't understand. How did Willow find out about the photos so quickly?"

I could tell by the way she looked at me that she

thought I knew the answer. And I did. Willow knew about the photos because Rex confessed to her. That's where he went when he left me in the kitchen on that clear, sunny afternoon. And why did he tell her? The only answer I could think of was both the sweetest and the saddest—in that moment of clarity he'd realized he truly loved her.

My heart sinks with sad irony. Poor Rex. By the time he woke up and did the right thing, it was too late. What a story *that* would make. It would be huge. A modern-day version of *Romeo and Juliet*.

"Any idea?" Carla asked.

I shook my head. "Not a clue."

She nodded slowly, as if to let me know she didn't believe me but that she accepted I had the right not to tell her. "So, I'm just curious," she said. "What *did* you do with those shots?"

I gazed up at the office wall, at the photos of all those famous people. Some famous for their talent. Some famous for their hard work and diligence. Some famous for outrageous acts and wanton flouting of the laws and conventions. Some famous merely for being famous. What was the one thing most of them now had in common? They'd been forgotten. Their moment had passed. They were no longer stars. You could call them has-beens, but to me that felt mean. Mostly they were part of an infinitesimal group of people who had, for a brief time and for whatever reason, experienced something rare—

real fame. But now they were just everyday people again. Davy once asked me if I thought it was better to be a has-been than a never was, but maybe it doesn't make all that much of a difference. In the end, people are just people, and the only things that matter are whether they are good or bad, loving or unloving, loved or unloved.

I realized that Carla hadn't said a word. She was gazing at me with a strange expression. "The shots on your camera?" she repeated in case I'd forgotten.

But, of course, I hadn't forgotten. I would never forget the crooked, unfocused images—the mirror lying face up on the table. The uneven lines of white powder. Willow's reflection—her eyes squeezed shut, bent over the mirror with a rolled-up bill pressed to her nostril.

"Erased them," I said.

There is a boy who is confined to a wheelchair. He cannot speak or make coherent gestures, but he is smart enough to make his feelings known. Most of the time it takes very little to make him happy. Just the attention of someone who cares about him, and perhaps a chance to go outside and feel the breeze on his skin and look at the clouds.

He has an older sister who is, in many ways, your typical, self-absorbed, uncertain and searching teenager. But maybe she's been lucky. She's learned something at an early age that many people may never learn.

It is an unusually crisp, clear afternoon in New York

City. The sky is blue except for some cottony white clouds here and there. Thanks to the bright sunlight and the clarity of the air, everything seems to be in extra-sharp focus—the feathery white edges of the clouds against the blue sky, the individual green leaves on the trees, even the cables that support the George Washington Bridge.

The boy's sister pushes him along a path in Riverside Park beside the Hudson River. She stops beside an empty bench and positions the wheelchair so that they can sit beside each other. The breeze lifts his fine hair, and the sun warms his face. They look out at the river, where a red and white tugboat pushes a barge upstream, and a small sailboat with a white sail tacks this way and that. The boy raises and drops his head in a way that makes his sister think he is trying to feel the breeze on every part of his face. She leans forward and turns to look at him. There is a crooked smile on his lips. He is overjoyed to be there, and to be with her. She places her hand over his and squeezes.

She can frame the shot in her mind. The two of them, the bench, the green trees behind them, the river before them, the clear light, the blue sky, the puffy white clouds. A beautiful shot, a singled-out moment of value to no one but them, an event that no paparazzi would ever bother to cover, concerning a young man hardly anyone knows.

But there will be no story about this moment, no photographs. No one except the two of them will ever know.

It is the best thing she can do.